HER PERFECT PLAN

HER PERFECT PLAN

ANURADHA GOSWAMI

Srishti
Publishers & Distributors

Srishti Publishers & Distributors
A unit of AJR Publishing LLP
212A, Peacock Lane
Shahpur Jat, New Delhi – 110 049

editorial@srishtipublishers.com

First published by
Srishti Publishers & Distributors in 2025

10 9 8 7 6 5 4 3 2 1

Printed and bound in India.

TO MY SON, SIDDHANT GOSWAMI

For seeing a book in me when even the thought had not crossed my mind.

For his desire to see my work in bookshops has actually manifested it.

For being my everyday cheerleader.

TO MY MOTHER

For opening doors to the most progressive world.

For introducing intellectually stimulating life filled with art and artists, literature and literati.

This book is a result of your teachings.

Chapter 1

The alarm went off, and Molina began counting.

One, two, three, four, five, six, seven… and the sound got muted.

She was downstairs in the kitchen and as soon as the alarm was shut, she began counting again and as she reached 'eighteen', right on dot, she heard her name being called out.

"Mols!"

Like clockwork. Every single day. At the same time, at the same count. Shutting off the alarm and at the same count, calling out her name.

Could life be any more predictable?

It was yet another morning of the usual robotic day – waking up and going about your life mechanically. Every household has a more or less similar routine and a similar calm and settled energy that enveloped the morning chaos. Everyone was busy starting their day with such precision that it could look like life was in repeat mode. Though every morning was a promise of a new day, we rarely ever stopped to feel, let alone enjoy and appreciate what seemed like a boring, stagnated life, but what, in reality, was a blessing. For in one second, everything could turn upside down, and one's life would never be the same again. And what looked like the same old, same old, we wish could have remained the same old. That same old monotonous morning could turn into one unforgettable one from which there was no return.

Molina and Sam woke up to a usual day. The morning cup of tea sipped mindlessly, eyes stuck to the newspaper, shifting now and then to the phone and back to the paper and then the phone again. The mind was already ready to get up and start the day, but the body was not yet cooperating. The hustle and bustle around the kitchen, bathroom, and dressing mirror. A shirt was being ironed, the toaster popping, eggs breaking, breakfast being laid, vitamins being counted, and tiffin being packed. The husband was arguing on the phone with a colleague or yelling at a subordinate while the wife chided the kids or house help. A hurried shower for some and an even more hurried breakfast for others. It was the time of the day when the woman of the house was far busier than any company head. They were at their multitasking best, and if there were children to attend to, it was a complete war zone. Yet there was a unique, blissful energy amidst the chaos that encircled the marital home of a happy family.

And what an irreparable loss to lose it all and to never find it again.

That fateful day, the house was going with the flow; she had less work on her hands. Their son Veer was at Molina's parents' house for the weekend, and they were to drop him off at school from there. She was the only child of her parents, and Veer was their only grandchild. Her parents, now retired and mostly home, couldn't have enough of Veer; their life revolved around him more than it had ever done around Molina, and she was thankful for the right balance it provided Veer and her. They both got their much-needed break away from each other. It gave her a lot of free time, not only to pursue her passion along with her home but also to relax with some 'me' time thrown in.

It was her morning alone with Sam. She sat down for a quick breakfast with him when Sam's phone rang. He looked at the phone, picked it up and started walking away, leaving his half-eaten breakfast.

Molina yelled, "Sam?"

She gestured towards the food. There was something about women and food, especially the food they lay out on the table. For them, the whole world stops functioning when they served food on the table. The fruit of their labour, in other words. And they become dictators. No distraction or interruption is allowed. They slog in the kitchen for it, and you are required to do full justice to it. And if appreciation for it follows, then you have totally won them over.

Sam lifted his hand, gesturing her to wait. Molina's arched eyebrows screamed, 'whatever'.

He headed towards the back lawn, talking animatedly on the phone. She watched him as he turned halfway back in and right out of the door, weakly murmuring, "I gotta go."

Molina looked at the shutting door and yelled again, "Sam? Sam!"

But the door was already shut after him. She rushed into the kitchen, came out, grabbed his lunch box and ran out in the hope that she might catch him. Sam, however, was nowhere in sight. A look of disbelief passed her face. Sam had left his lunch? It was strange enough that he had left his breakfast half eaten, but leaving his lunch behind was not Sam. With his acute acidity and ulcer concerns, eating out was not an option and skipping a meal was a big no-no. What was the tearing hurry? She wondered, as she leisurely walked back into the house, confused and worried. She tried calling him. Maybe he could send someone from the office to pick it up. No answer. Tried again. Nada.

Now what? Would she have to go up to his office to drop it? She was mulling over it when suddenly the doorbell rang.

A look of relief waved through her face like a cold breeze. She knew Sam couldn't have gone too far before realizing that in his hurry to leave, he had forgotten his lunch.

"Silly man," Molina uttered, shaking her head. With a lifted brow and lopsided smile, she opened the door.

However, standing there was Urvashi. Her childhood friend, her only support in the town, her only family here, so to say. Inadvertently, her face screamed disappointment and her unwelcoming body remained reactionless to Urvi's approaching arms. Urvi took a step back to study the unbelievable sight.

She looked Molina up and down.

"Wow. Someone is really super excited to see her bestie. Good to see you too," she said sarcastically.

There was no reaction.

"What's going on? Wrong time? Definitely the wrong person! What's going on?"

Urvi looked at her curiously.

"Huh?" Molina was still in a daze.

Her eyes were searching far and beyond Urvi. And her mind was trying to bring back Sam. Partly because she wanted him to have this lunch and, more importantly, because she really hated going to his office. The Sam there was never her Sam. She felt she was an intruder in his busy world, where there was no place or time for idle chatter and pleasantries. He was always curt and in a hurry to get rid of her. And without saying as much, he always succeeded in convincing her that it was a bad idea for her to be there.

"Hello… where are we lost?"

"Oh… sorry… sorry… I am so sorry, Urvi, my darling…" Molina finally said as if woken up from her trance, as she looked into her eyes apologetically.

"I'm really sorry. And when am I ever not happy to see you?" she stressed, holding her hands.

"Oh, just shut up. I know the happy look, and I know the sad look. In fact, I know all your looks. Now tell me, whom were you expecting at the door? Huh?"

She had a mockingly playful look on her face, "Secret lover, hmmm?" Urvi teased.

"Keep going, face reader. What else didn't you miss? And when you are done, tell me when I can get my comforting hug."

"Awwwww," went Urvi and soon the besties were hugging each other with lifted spirits.

"Look at this." Molina signalled to the tiffin in her hands. "Sam Sir left in such a hurry that he left his breakfast untouched and forgot his lunch. I thought he had returned to pick it up. And I will now have to go drop it off," she sighed. "You have no idea how I hate to go to his workplace!" She threw her hands up. "Anyway, tell me what we are having. Green tea or coffee?"

She grinned and pinched Urvi's cheeks. The doting friend was back.

Relaxed, Molina slumped on the sofa. She could use a bit of a sit-down and chitchat with her bestie.

"So, tell me, what was that? You seriously seemed full of doubts. Are you insecure? Really? Since when?" Molina teased her friend, not noticing that Urvi was still standing restlessly.

"I don't know. Emotions change. People are unpredictable and confusing. Anyway, with you, I was just pulling your leg. You know you can't get rid of me, not in this lifetime, maybe not even after," Urvi quipped.

"Good girl," Molina said approvingly. "Don't ever question my love and loyalty. Once I love, it's for keeps. And if you happen to change, then God help you, 'cause it won't be pretty," Molina said in jest.

But who knew that the words would hold true in the days to come?

With her head resting on the lifted cushion, she stretched her legs onto the coffee table in front of her.

"No, no! No one is sitting here and no one is having any coffee or tea. You get up right now and put some decent clothes on. Come on, get up… fast… fast…. Hurry up." Urvi said as she suddenly remembered why she was there.

"Hey, I am dressed decently, okay? What's this now? Dress decent? You mean this is indecent?" Molina sat up, startled.

"Hello relax, what's with you today? Why are your claws out? Not my fault that your thirty-seven year old baby forgot his Cerelac!"

Urvi sounded pissed.

"I am asking you to get up and get dressed," she continued. "But wait, you don't even want to know why… right? Now, could you please not pick on every word and actually listen to me?" she added in a huff.

Molina got up. She went straight to Urvi and embraced her.

"I am being a bitch, aren't I?" She made a remorseful face. "Please do tell me, my dear friend. I am all ears now."

Molina released Urvi from her arms. She started making her way to the kitchen to make them some coffee.

"Hey, come back! Where do you think you are going, Mols? I am asking you to hurry up and come with me, and you are taking a walk in the park! With your pace, I might just end up delivering my baby here!"

Urvi's frustration got the better of her, and she let the cat out of the bag. This was not how she wanted to break the news to her best friend. She had rung the doorbell with so much excitement, waiting to make a dramatic entry as the door opened. She had rehearsed the screenplay in her mind all the way to the house. She thought she would play around the prodding about why she was there so early. She then, purposely to tease her curious friend, would give vague excuses. Followed by a suspenseful pause before she would get down to make the theatrical announcement of the happiest day of her life, jump on her friend and yell with glee that she was soon going to be a… yes… a… mom! She was pregnant, and their wait – Urvi's, her husband Jay's, and Molina's – was over, and their prayers had finally been answered.

***

It had taken six long years of planning and trying, keeping dreams on hold, and pushing plans aside to achieve the biggest one. It was a long wait of months of anxiety and suspense, the fear of failure and disappointment, the struggle to not lose hope and the need for a strong heart to not give up and keep trying. It was not just that she was finally pregnant; it was a battle she had finally won.

It was a war with her body from which she had emerged victorious. It was getting a glimpse of the other side of the mighty peak of hope and swimming to the other side of the never-ending ocean of treatments. It was her moment. And she needed her moment to be colossal. But here she was, breaking the news impetuously and so out of context. Nevertheless, the effect was just what she would have wanted.

"What did you say? Say that again… Oh my god! Yes... oh yes… oh yes! We did it… We did it… we did it."

And yes, it was no less than 'we did it' for Urvi and Molina.

As the news settled, Molina realized what a total disaster she had made of the moment. To compare a forgotten lunch box fiasco to the biggest life-changing announcement was inexcusable. She found herself feeling utterly foolish and cheap, not to mention unpardonably guilty.

What was wrong with her? Why was she such a babysitter to her family? Why was every missed beat in the house her problem, even if it was not? For the first time, she felt she had to loosen the grip so those who were hanging from it could learn to balance their act. She was an over-obsessive wife, mother and homemaker. She had to admit it. It was okay as far as her six-year-old son Veer was concerned. He was a baby, still waking up to the world. Her indulgence toward him was needed. Not the rest, though. To hell with Sam's lunch. He was a grown man, and she should have let him sort it out.

"Hello. Shall we? We still have to go see my gynaecologist and get a confirmation."

She found Urvi's snapping fingers flash before her eyes.

"I have just done a home test, by the way. I didn't want to tell Jay till it was a 'yes' from the doctor. You know how fragile he gets every single time. His guilt about me being the bearer of the physical torment is killing him anyway. I thought I should spare him the disappointment, just in case. With you, I know I can pile on any nonsense and won't bat an eyelid, so here I am." She winked and hurried her again, "Come on now, hurry!"

Molina's plastered smile was getting wider by the minute. She swung into action, declaring, "I'll be right back in the most appropriate ensemble for an aunt. Am going to be 'the one' to look up to."

She left to get dressed.

***

Urvi paced up and down the room. Her heart was in her mouth, and she needed it to slide back to its place, for it had a lot coming its way. As she saw Molina emerge from her room, she gestured to her to get moving and waited till Molina stepped ahead of her so Urvi could follow her out.

Molina took over as they reached her car and insisted that she drive. Urvi didn't argue. Anything to reach the doctor at the earliest. As they sat down, Molina realized Urvi was suddenly obeying her unquestioningly. That was quite unlike her. She could make out that she was tense. She felt the urgency in the air and glanced at Urvi reassuringly.

"Don't you worry, I've got it!" she said and drove out to the main road.

Slightly relaxed now, Urvi couldn't help but comment, "Aren't you a tad overdressed for a clinic visit? And it's a gynaecologist's clinic, where frumpy fat women are waiting in their oversized clothes. Don't you think it's kind of unfair to them to look so damn gorgeous and sexy? And what if their men are accompanying them? You will make it hellish for them with their men ogling at you. And they will, trust me."

"That's the idea," Molina joined in light-heartedly. "You won't understand, darling. I am over the moon, not overdressed. The child needs to learn to be stylish right now. And who better to learn from?"

Even before the car came to a complete halt, Urvi jumped out and said, "Park and come in. I'll go and get an appointment."

Of course, thought Molina.

***

CHAPTER 2
THE CLINIC AND THE CLICHÉ

It took some time before Molina could find an empty spot. Looking at the number of cars parked, she knew it was going to be quite a wait. She walked towards the building and then took a detour towards a nearby Starbucks. She remembered her untouched cup of coffee lying somewhere in the house, totally forgotten amidst the morning's madness. Her morning coffee was her mood lifter, her spirit enhancer, and her body fuel. Right now, she sure could certainly use all of that. She went in and picked up an Americano for herself and a cold coffee for Urvi. It's the only thing Urvi could have in the name of coffee. She was a masala chai person.

As she stepped into the lobby of the building, she hoped there was someone near the elevator to call for it as she had both her hands full. She didn't have to wait long. A middle-aged couple came right behind her and pressed the button.

She said, "Thanks."

The man gave a wide smile in acknowledgement. Men are at their courtliest best with an unknown woman. As if painting on an empty canvas, they have the power to choose how the form unfolds.

"This cold one is for my friend," she said, pointing towards the bigger cup and immediately felt foolish. Who was asking? She asked herself.

"Was wondering." Never to lose an opportunity, the man joined in the irrelevant conversation. "Hot and cold together? Not unless you crush after a dentist."

He laughed at his own joke. Molina managed a polite smile. She had started it, so she'd better suffer now.

"So, your friend is up there already?" Pleased with himself, he continued.

"Must be some really impatient patient." Seeing no response, he smiled and added as an afterthought, "This one was bad."

"Both were," the woman with him coolly tried to shut him up and winked at Molina.

"I may not know you, but I already love you," Molina said, looking at the woman as the elevator came to a halt.

Inside the waiting area, there were more people standing than sitting. She inspected the crowd, looking for Urvi, and found her standing near the water cooler, filling a glass of water. She walked up to her and handed the cold coffee. "Forget water. Here, I got you this."

"Oh, thank you so much. I was dying of boredom. This is my third glass of water. Imagine drinking water to pass the time. A first definitely," she cribbed. "Glad I jumped out and came rushing in. Guess how many people filled in after me? Seven! Can you believe it? I saved us over an hour or maybe even much more, you know," she gloated.

"Always the smart one." And Molina let her.

"Still, it looks like quite a wait, I would say."

Molina, not being used to staying idle, suggested, "Shall we play cross and zero? I am sure I will have a pad and pen in this luggage of mine." She pointed to her humongous shoulder bag.

"Good idea."

"Would you happen to have a blanket somewhere in there?" Urvi added teasingly, and then rubbing her folded arms for warmth, complained, "This place is freaking freezing. And that bloody patient has been in there like forever," she said. Just then the door opened.

Her eyes lit up for a second, and then they froze. And in that moment, she knew that their life would never be the same again.

****

Urvi stared at the face that had just walked out the door, and the face stared back at her. There was no escaping. There was no hiding. She saw him, and she saw him looking back at her. She struggled to find her breath and feel her limbs and to find her senses, but it seemed like the very life had fled out of her. Her mind went numb, her body motionless, and her face turned ashen as though she had seen a ghost.

"Here," Molina flashed the pad in front of her face and challenged, "Each set 100? Cool? Why not make some money while we are at it," she said playfully and looked at Urvi, expecting her to protest but found herself looking at Urvi's ashen face. Her eyes had a faraway look and horror written all over it. Her eyes followed Urvi's gaze. And the sight she beheld would lead to her world crumbling.

Standing there was Sam. Sam, holding the hand of a heavily pregnant woman. Holding the hand of a woman she had never seen before.

No one moved. No one could. It seemed like time had stood still.

There are situations in your lives when your mind and body refuse to cooperate, coordinate and correlate with each other. While the body goes into a static state like a carcass, the mind, in contrast, races up like a wayward wind blowing in all directions. As if taking the whole responsibility of pulling us out of the disarray, it instructs the body not to make any move. Or, like the body is washing its hands off by telling the mind that it's your mess, you go deal with it.

The hand that Sam was holding was freed, but his feet were fixed on the floor as if they were nailed onto it. His entire being was crushing under the weight of the two pairs of eyes. Guilt mixed with shame and fear enveloped Sam as he saw an inevitable end to one part of his dual life. He was standing there, stripped of his lies. He knew he was doomed.

On the part of the girls, they were just spectators to the drama that was unfolding in front of them. Though it must have felt like an eternity, it mustn't have been long before the bell for the next patient rang, and the stupor was broken. And the woman with him made the first move. She had little to lose, so she came around fast. Sensing the complexities of the situation, she decided she had to make her presence felt. She didn't need to stand in attendance to let these three decide her fate. This wasn't her battleground, and this wasn't her fight. It was in her favour as the cat was out of the bag, and she couldn't be happier.

She looked at Sam and though lightly pulled his hand in a manner that suggested that they should get going, Sam didn't budge.

He tried to read Molina's face and her mind; he tried to read her. There she was, his friend, his lover and his wife standing in front of him, standing amongst the strangers and blending with them as if she were one of them. She didn't seem like the woman he woke up next to that morning; the woman he had been waking up next to morning after morning. Instead, there stood someone who came from somewhere unknown and might just disappear into the unknown. And he wouldn't be able to see where. It seemed as though the darkness of his betrayal descended between them, and it dawned upon him that it wouldn't be easy finding his way through the darkness. He feared he might get lost and never reach the other side. The darkness was too thick, too heavy, and too frightening.

At that moment, it struck him. She was the woman he loved; she was the only woman he had ever loved. And he might have just lost her. He could feel the bulk of his philandering ways finally crushing him under its weight and, along with it, his house, his life, and his happiness. If he could see any emotion, any flicker of a sign, he would reach out and receive his sentence. He would risk every breath of his life to douse the fire that was burning her. Their years of togetherness had made him familiar with her soft spots, her vulnerabilities. He could read every fold, every crease on her face and knew what went on behind them. He was searching for any tell-tale sign of shock, anger, hurt, hatred, disgust, sadness, helplessness, and tears. Something… anything. But there was none. She was as dead as they come.

She was looking at him. She was looking right into his eyes but she wasn't seeing him; she was seeing someone else standing there. Her doors were shut on him.

The hand was pulling him now with a certain tenacity. As if forcing a decision on him. As if claiming ownership of him. As if ascertaining authority on him.

All three sets of eyes were on him. Which way would he go? Who would he choose?

And in just that moment, he made the stupidest, meanest, and cruellest call of this life. He let himself get dragged out of the place by that hand.

***

There could be many different interpretations of that decision. But there can never be any justification. On his part, he must have weighed the favourable action, given the place and situation. They were in a nursing home where many knew him. He may have wanted to avoid any confrontation and drama that would follow if he had tried to make any amends, as if there could have been any scope to make amends, to begin with. Molina was just not there. Her physical form was visible to the eyes, but his Molina, whom he knew, was nowhere around. Even if he had left the woman and walked up to her, the woman would not have taken it kindly. There would have been screaming, shouting, abusing and maybe even cursing. With everything lost at one end and too much to deal with at the other, his foggy brain and his terrified heart made the clouded judgment. And so, like a coward, he silently left with the woman.

Sam didn't realize it, but at that moment, he made the decision for Molina.

Her Sam was here. She couldn't have been dreaming. She could swear it was him. She knew her Sam; she could spot him amongst any number of people. But if it was Sam, what was he doing here? Why had he left without meeting her? And what was he doing with that strange woman? Why was he holding her hand? Wasn't that woman full-blown pregnant? Yes, she was. She was with a child. And he was holding her hand. Was she with his child? She was with his child. He was holding her hand. And he walked out holding her hand.

She was with his child. He walked out with her.

He can't be her Sam.

She has no Sam.

There is no Sam.

Urvi could only dare to look at Molina through the corner of her eyes. She sat there in silence, icy cold silence that pierced through her bones. She was alive, but she had died. She was breathing, but there was no life. Urvi's initial shock started turning into a rage – an overpowering, uncontrollable, violent, abusive rage. And then guilt and self-blame started replacing her anger. It was her doing, in a way. She had misplaced her trust, and she had miscalculated. If it were she in place of Molina, she would have expected her friend to tell her the truth. She would have traded that pain for this. A small wound compared to this lethal cut?

Any day

***

CHAPTER 3
MOLINA

She was just different. And here is why. Most of us are who we are, not because we try to be a certain way but because we are a certain way. Good, bad, ugly – we are what we are, and then we add some. Watch and learn, see and imbibe, follow some, reject others. We see judgments being made, rules being imposed, and standards being set. Either we go along like a leaf floating in the water wherever the current takes it, or we become the water and take our own course. Those who rebel do so because they don't agree, they don't confirm, and they just don't get it.

And then there are those who aren't paying any attention to the complexities – human or otherwise. Their canvas is plain and simple. It's only them, and then there is nature. Humans are invisible and unimportant, not out of hatefulness or dislike but because they bring nothing into their world. It's like when you are looking through a lens, and you focus on the background, the foreground turns blurry. In Molina's life lens, people would blur, conversations would go mute, and nothing would get noticed or registered. People were all the same, all the time, everywhere. Her focus was the background. The background was always interesting. It changed constantly and beautifully, and it brought happiness. And Molina was happy. She was always happy. She was a die-hard romantic, and she remained dreamy-eyed. She walked around dazed, but she was more aware of the world than most because she saw what others couldn't. She felt what the others couldn't. And she loved what others didn't.

What remained of the rest of the world, she obliged with occasional attention and kindness whenever it was needed. And lived forbearingly and gratified.

She was always different.

As a little girl, Molina was a timid child. As the only child of her parents, she was not confident in a crowd and almost always stuck only to her best friend, Urvi, from the neighbourhood. Less was more for her, and she knew no better than that, as she was born into a nuclear family of three. Her world had been small from day one. She wasn't born a privileged kid. She didn't have it all. In fact, she had very little. Hers was a deprived childhood in more ways than one. Her parents loved her but had very little time for her. Both were working long hours to make ends meet. Her father was a government clerk and was paid a pittance. He was responsible for maintaining the files at the office of the railway ministry, and his job had plenty of opportunities to demand bribes. It was given that clerks made their fair share of money by pay-offs, and hence, their salary was never a subject of consideration. Molina's father, however, fell on the other side of corruption and suffered at the hands of his honesty. Her mother was a nurse for elderly women, tending to them at their homes and had been looking after a lonely woman for nine years. She had got the job through an agency. Most of what she got paid was kept by the agency guy, and she was handed over very little of it. But she didn't complain as she felt safe there, and the lady of the house was kind to her and Molina. She used to be a poor but exceptionally good-looking young girl, and she had to endure a lot of unwanted and undesirable male encounters. It resulted in her withdrawing into a shell and making her fearful of the men of the world. She opted to be around women, and the older, the better. Her poverty and her innocence combined proved to be a handicap, and she didn't have the heart to fight the vultures in the big bad world.

And the man she married didn't help to boost her courage. He was too gentlemanly and dignified a soul and could never bring out any aggression, even when men openly made a pass at his wife. He found solace in the fact that he had what others wanted and settled for the feeling of gratitude for the privilege of having such a desirable woman for a wife. He had avoided bullies all his life, and he advised her to do so as well. And the decision was made for her. She was to work privately and had the liberty to accept or reject the job offers depending on the safety of the workplace. Being a qualified nurse, she found that home jobs suited her best.

Of whatever the couple could make, which wasn't much, they managed to save up enough for a house of their own, her education and of course her wedding.

The birth of a daughter followed a saving scheme, especially in India. A good groom came with a price at most times. If you were lucky, you might get chosen for your qualities, but only if you were lucky. As for the rest, the more money you wanted your daughter to enjoy, the more you had to spend to secure it. A well-earning husband was the woman's decided goal. So, money was being saved for Molina so that she could get married into money. They had seen the side of poverty and wanted Molina to lead a far better life.

She was dearly loved at home, but money and her parents' time were always in short supply. Molina had learnt to live with just love. Stubborn tantrums, insistent demands and materialistic indulgences were not part of her childhood and that made her easy-going and loving. To compensate for the lack of everything else, her parent's life, whenever home, revolved only around her. Very early in life, she learnt about quality over quantity, and as she grew, she too chose to follow the same. She chose few, and she gave them her all.

She was average in studies, poor in sports, and disinterested in extracurricular activities; there didn't seem to be any promising career ahead of her. Her parents often prodded her about what she wanted to be when she grew up, but she never wanted to look so far ahead. She lived in the moment, and she never felt the need to get out of it to search for something that was still unknown: the future.

While her parents were at work, she had her dolls to play with. From a very early age, her dolls became her family, and she set up a house with them. In the absence of money, she made her dolls herself at home. It all began with her putting together rags of old clothes and sewing them into the shape of a doll that she had seen at the roadside stall. She managed to make a fairly good one. Being happy and satisfied with it, she began improvising.

They were not fancy dolls you could buy from shops, but she knew no better so she loved them. She started celebrating festivals with them and dressing them up, adding variety to her collection. With that her imagination soared, she began to create beautiful clothes and accessories for them from whatever she could find around the house. She created clothes from plastic bags, paper wrappers, and old fabrics. She made beautiful jewellery from threads and beads and whatever she could lay her hands on.

Slowly it became her passion. She set about to improvise the way the dolls were made and soon she had very pretty dolls in her collection. They were not just pretty they were different from other dolls in the market. They were unique and very attractive.

***

When something grows in front of your eyes, bit by bit, you seldom take notice of the larger picture till someone points it out to you. A similar thing happened to Molina's growing talent. Her parents were oblivious to the level she had reached in terms of her creativity. They were happy and impressed with what they would see every few days and kept encouraging her by constantly patting her on her back. But it started and ended with a typical parental nod. They didn't make much of it. Their daughter was just playing with her dolls in her spare time, and that kept her happy. It was when one of her dolls, by the chance of fate, landed in the hands of her schoolteacher that they woke to their daughter's extraordinary talent. Molina was eleven years old when, on Urvi's birthday, she decided to part with her best doll as a gift for her best friend.

It wasn't a well-thought-out birthday gift wrapped in decorative paper with a note declaring love and good wishes. She wasn't holding it behind her back to surprise Urvi when she walked in with slices of her birthday cake for Molina's parents. She was just sitting and lovingly staring at her latest and most perfect doll. As Urvi arrived, Mols innocently showed her her new creation. They were best friends, and it was their common shared pleasure. Urvi held the doll in her hands and squealed with excitement. She hugged it and kept kissing it as if she had the world in her hands. At that moment, something in Molina said to her that she wouldn't be able to love the doll as much as Urvi did. She very softly and decisively said, "You take it. It's yours."

For Urvi, it was a birthday gift from her bestie. Her mom had gifted her her first lipstick, her dad bought her a bicycle, and her aunt had a bunch of pretty hair accessories. So, when Molina handed her the brand-new doll, it seemed like one more gift for her special day. And in the excitement of showing off what she got for her birthday, Urvi stuffed her assorted gifts in her school bag to flaunt to her classmates. It was while the bunch of girls were bending over the gifts that one of the boys from their class jumped over and snatched the doll. He playfully ran off with it. Urvi ran after him, yelling and crying. The boy picked up speed and ran out of the class into the corridor, and that's where he collided with the approaching teacher. And the doll fell out of his hand onto the floor.

The teacher's eyes followed the gaze of the boy, and it took them to the lying object in front of her. Just as she was trying to figure out what was going on, a distraught and crying Urvi came running, and without noticing the teacher and the slowly collecting crowd, she stopped and sat on the floor clutching her doll. The case was solved. The doll belonged to Urvi, and the boy had run away with it to tease the girl.

It was in the principal's office that the story of the origin of the doll came about. They learned that Molina was the maker of the doll gifted to Urvi. Urvi had brought it to school as she wanted everyone to see how talented her friend was (Urvi tried to save her skin). What could have been just a broken rule of sneaking in a personal item became a cause, and what could have got her punishment made her a noble soul.

From being a matter of disciplinary action, it became a responsibility to encourage the hidden talent of a poor student on the principal's part. The principal looked at the doll with admiration. It wasn't every day that a gifted student was discovered in their institute. And someone with such unique and innovative craftsmanship had never certainly been seen. Not only in her school but anywhere else that she knew of. The clever use of waste material with such intricate detail immediately made her a fan of

Molina. She knew not only that Molina was on the way to success and recognition, but that she and her school would be famous soon.

The principal summoned Molina and the teacher. Urvi was sent back to her class. Molina stood frozen. Her little heart was engulfed with fear as she stood in front of the principal. Her feeble mind was filled with the possibilities of the most terrifying punishment. She didn't look up. She couldn't. Hers was a life very specifically chalked out by dos and don'ts. And she followed it to the T. There was no extended family, no cousins, and no gang of mischievous friends to influence or instigate her to break any rules. She did what she was told to do. And she was told, like the rest of the students, that none of their personal belongings were allowed on the school premises. She forgot that she hadn't brought it in. She just heard her name being mentioned in the same breath as the doll, and the sweet, fragile kid in her overcame with such unimaginable anguish as if the life had left her body.

She couldn't hold it in any longer and everything that was melting inside, found a way out through the burst of overflowing tears. She was trembling and incessantly weeping, but all so silently that it took a while for the teachers to realize that their able student was oblivious to the turn of events. They also realized that not only was Molina exceptionally skillful, but immensely meek and clueless as well.

The principal got up from her chair of authority and did something that she had never done in her career. She walked up to the shaking, sobbing, petrified kid and took her in her arms. She encircled her with comforting assurance and wiping her tears, she whispered in her ears, "You are here because you are a very special girl; because you are better than others, because we love you for your pretty dolls."

Not one to look for any kind of attention, Molina couldn't fathom what it was all about. Though a little comforted by the hug and kind words, she was only longing to go home to her mother. Since it was not going to be anything bad after all, it was more than enough for her. No thought of appreciation, award or glory crossed her mind. The security of her home was all she needed. A faint "home" and "mom" were all she managed to say.

Their experienced minds knew there was no getting across to the kid. They would have to take it up with the mother another day. The matter was kept aside to pursue at a later date. A milkshake was ordered for Molina, and while they waited, the principal looked into her drawer, hoping to find something among her knick-knacks to gift Molina to appease her. A brooch gleamed at the top of the drawer, and it was quickly pinned to the white collar of her uniform. Two things were achieved. First, the kid was finally assured that she was not in any trouble, and secondly, once she stepped out, the school and its denizens would be assured, too. And she would not be mocked by her fellow students. The principal now knew she was too meek a girl and did not have it in her to deal with cruel bullies.

***

Molina became the principal's pet project. There was something about a teacher's love and indulgence towards outstanding students. As soon as a glimmer of anything exceptional about a kid was noticed, they took it as their life's goal to make sure that it reached its maximum potential. Rules were broken for them, concessions were made, and preferences were given. All in all, they got a VIP pass for anything related to school.

It was on that fateful day that the faceless, nameless little girl became the poster girl of the school. The doll was put on display, first in the teacher's room for them to give their opinions and suggestions and later at the entrance of the dining hall for the children's response. And as expected, it proved to be a big draw. The dining was abuzz with soft murmurs somewhere and loud natter elsewhere. But one thing was clear: everyone had something to say about it.

It was later decided that Molina didn't have it in her to fathom the magnitude of this mammoth opportunity. Her parents needed to be summoned. But it was again a cause for concern to ask Molina to get her parents to school. The kid had barely managed to shake off the all-encompassing fear, and telling her to get her parents to school might just alter that. So, it was decided that they would make a personal visit to her home. The two school authorities decided on the appropriate day and time and set out on their mission. What was happening was nothing less than the force of nature, for what was being taken as the topmost priority by the two could have been just left as an everyday occurrence between classmates. But it was willed to have a life ahead.

Seeing the principal at the door, even Molina's father skipped a heartbeat, but it was restored immediately as he heard them saying,

"We are here to encourage your daughter. You have an exceptionally artistic kid, and it was only befitting to congratulate you both in person. So here we are."

They were invited in by smiling faces and straightened backs. There was no happiness compared to that which came from the achievements of your child. Even the most humble and unassuming parent's chest swelled with pride. And Molina's parents couldn't have been prouder because their little girl had self-invented, self-improved and self-mastered the craft she was being noticed for. What made the undertaking even more vital to pursue was the fact that it was apparent the girl's family was in dire straits. Money was scarce, the basic necessities were met with great difficulties, and childhood was devoid of any frills or trappings. To cultivate and flourish amongst these circumstances at this young age, the child was further elevated in their eyes, and a decision was made instantly that not only would the talent of the kid be encouraged, but monetary benefits had to be considered as well.

A proposition was made that Molina would continue with her playful hobby as usual, without any extra pressure or undue expectations, so that the child didn't lose her freedom to use her hours as she would. However, efforts would be made to make sure that her creativity was kept alive and that opportunities were given to her to improve her craft further. It was suggested that her creations were good enough to be exhibited at various interschool events and competitions and should be promoted at children's stores and bookshops. Local newspapers were also considered for publishing articles about her skills using waste material and creating awareness about recycling consciousness among young children with the help of the little beauties. And if her parents were not opposed to it, they could help her sell them at a really good price and let her make her own money.

So Molina was not to have any change of routine. The change was to come in the form of rewards. Her entire education expenditure was to be taken care of by the school, and the money that her work generated would go into her education fund for higher studies. There was an objective to this arrangement. The scholarship proposal was to keep the parents interested and involved. And the fund was to secure her future when she got out from under their wings. The aspect of financial benefit was totally lost on Molina as she was too young to realize that fortune was suddenly smiling in her backyard. Instead, the faces smiling at her lifted her spirits and confidence, motivated her to create more and more.

***

CHAPTER 4
FRUITFUL FATE

And so, her journey towards a promising vocation began. Soon her dolls were talking points at the school amongst parents, and even at social gatherings. Many competing parents suddenly woke up, and requests started pouring in from parents, to make their kids also learn the fine art of doll-making under the supervision of Molina.

It started with one or two mothers, who would come to pick their kids after school was over. They would wait and approach any teacher passing by, with some excuse or the other. And it would eventually end up that their child if given an opportunity, could be another Molina for school.

It was by the end of the academic year that things began looking up for Molina. Her habit of passing time doing this and that with her dolls became her passion. And as explained to her by her parents, she knew now that it helped them with the money for her schooling. Her little mind understood that this had relieved her Ma and Pa of at least some of their worries. She constantly reminded herself that she had to study hard as she had to justify the scholarship and, at the same time, continue with her work. All of this worked out in her favour. The girl who was far behind in her studies began catching up and became determined to succeed academically, too. At home, Ma and Pa always seemed to be in a good mood. The food was better, and she had nicer clothes. Ma often even took a day off, and they'd go to watch movies. Though she was not an attention seeker, the sudden love and affection that was bestowed upon her made her self-assured and approachable. This was the time she took her first step outside of her world.

And she began noticing a little, at least.

In all of this, the person who was unknowingly responsible for the entire development was left behind. Urvi's act of trying to save her skin, with a quick withdrawal from the scene that day, made everybody forget about her. She, on her part, was beyond relieved. In her little mind, Molina did her a big favour by not mentioning her name in connection to the episode. And it never occurred to her, even in later years, that it was she who had made Molina the star. Initially, out of guilt, she started helping Molina with the dolls, as she believed it was because of her that Molina had been taken to task by the principal. She had no idea about the arrangement between the elders, so she took the onus on herself to comfort her friend and lend a hand.

And a team was formed.

***

They worked and played at the same time, and their joint venture brought out more creative ideas. Soon, little furniture took shape, and then some utensils. Urvi had a little brother, so they made a He-man, a G.I. Joe and other figures for him. She was super excited and jubilant. She had come in as a helping hand and was now becoming a co-creator. Her suggestions were not only considered but implemented, too. Soon, two heads, instead of one, took the whole enterprise to another level. The more they were applauded for their natural and eco-friendly creations, the more they got inventive. Most materials came from recycled materials and were devoid of any hazardous components. They even started a toy library where used toys were donated by the wealthy for circulation amongst the poor kids. It became a craze, and they came in demand. Their bond, too, became stronger.

Many of the mothers would drop their daughters off at Molina's house under some pretext or another. They secretly wished that this way their child would be occupied constructively and be around a good influence by forming a close friendship with her. Suddenly, she was in demand socially. This helped the shy, meek and self-effacing little girl to open up. She talked a bit more, laughed a little louder, stepped outdoors often and grew more interested in life outside of the house and school. She was coming into her own. It was the enriching occurrences happening in her life that then brought about another change. Just as with this overwhelming recognition and kindness, her life had taken such a joyful turn, the same could be extended to other even lesser privileged kids, and more cheer could be spread.

The first hand that she held was of Urvi's domestic help's daughter, Noor. Her compassionate eyes didn't miss the yearning in Noor's eyes every time she came anywhere near Molina and Urvi. She was also around their age and had the same wants and wishes. So, one fine day, she was gently given a doll to hold. A while later, the hesitancy on both sides turned into familiarity, and Noor became Molina's second helping hand. She was rewarded with something or the other, and by herself learning about the pleasure of receiving, Molina also learned the pleasure of giving. Around the time she turned thirteen, she was asked to sew her own name on the back of her toys so as to establish the authenticity of her work. The heavy demand for them resulted in some more keen volunteers, and many needy little hands joined in. It was the perfect mix of play and purpose.

In days to come, how big would it get could be nobody's guess.

***

CHAPTER 5
COMING OF AGE

Now into her own, Molina stood tall at 5 feet 7" with a lithe body and a composed demeanour. It seemed as if she took her leisurely time to go about and often appeared unrushed, but her pace was fast. Not hurried, just fast. Those who got a chance to walk alongside her would be initially in disbelief at how they had to struggle to match her steps while she effortlessly marched ahead. Maybe it was her inner calm that covered her steps, but it was interestingly strange. And not just in steps but in life too – she could slickly achieve a lot more than most hasty ones.

She had a face which did not have perfect features if one looked at each feature separately. But together, it was a face that stood out and won over many prettier ones in a room. Many credited her long, soft curls fetchingly framing her face as the reason for instantly isolating her from the sea of similar frames, but she still drew eyes towards her even when she had her hair all tied up. And then, she had the sincerest eyes anyone had ever seen. They never searched the room for opportunities when she entered. They just greeted whoever they met, and then her smile took over, and then her warmth. She was an instant hit with most around her. On rare occasions, it did ignite sparks of jealousy or at least feelings of discomfort for those who compared. She had a posture that was angled more frontward from the waist up and could be judged as a sign of someone who is ever so willing to please and accommodate.

And on a broader scale, that could hold true. She had it in her to go the extra mile to understand a situation, a conversation or a person with an open mind and reasoning. But she also had it in her to outrightly reject something or someone at a glance and never think of giving it a chance.

If there was a room full of people chatting away their hearts out, she preferred to sit as an audience from a fairly interesting and entertaining spot from where she viewed and ascertained the marvel called humans. The varied faces, with enormous capacity to tirelessly indulge in chatter that didn't matter, the exchange of knowledge which never came from expertise or facts, the advice which was given but never taken, it was all a part of the theatrical that must have been unfolding from time immemorial. There always were certain defined types who took centre stage and held court. Then, the rest segregated into keen listeners, some actual believers, some not fully convinced and some outright cynics. She fell into none. She would be observing, and depending on the height of idiocies and inanity, she would sympathize with their compulsive need to participate in these futile encores, or she would silently question her own self lack of such need.

She derived a lot of pleasure from her silent observations of the life and people playing out in front of her and wouldn't want to change that for anything but the occasional doubt would creep in to speculate if all was well with her, to begin with. She was not sure which side was the right side – hers or theirs – and this turmoil definitely contributed in making her a bit uncertain and wondering about her lone spot.

And because of being the odd one out in the way she thought and believed, she had a hidden critic inside of herself about her own self. It wasn't apparent or obvious, but there was a layer of uncertainty that popped its head time and again and thus kept her from overvaluing herself. It made her unassuming and unassertive.

It kept her humble and human.

It helped her remain accessible and pleasant.

And it was like a cherry on the cake.

A perfect magnetic mélange.

***

There are some who, at best, can only be second best. Not that they lacked where others scored. In fact, sometimes or maybe often, they could outshine or outdo most, but the sheer disinterest in the valueless validation from others and the indifference to the worthless applause that was sought by the others made them backbenchers. Urvi was one such backbencher. For the wise and evolved, the back of the room always had the most to offer. You could pick and choose where you needed to look and what you wanted to hear. The eyes were not on you, but it worked for Urvi. She hated attention because she hated the intentions behind the attention. She could never enjoy a superior position or a prime spot, no matter what her feats or triumphs were. Because none qualified to stand superior to anyone, irrespective of where they came from and where they reached.

On a very practical and logical level, the adored and admired, respected and overpaid were not the ones needed for day-to-day requirements. It was the faceless and anonymous ones who brought the food on your table, water in your pot and a stitch to cover your modesty. Those who toil so we don't have to were the indispensable ones, the significant ones, the eligible ones for honour, if not for worship. Those who kept us alive.

But sadly, they remained the most uncared and unappreciated while the celebrated and revered were for pure delights entertainment. Their dream-like world and dazzling gloss blinded all. No one paused to think if they actually matter for the greater good.

This questionable divide and this thoughtless practice were so effectively disturbing for Urvi that she determinedly shunned to be on the other side. She stayed and flourished with the unknown. She wanted to live common, because common ran the world. She preferred to be in the shadow because the shadows soothed her.

And that was why Urvi was with Molina. She preferred to be the second best.

***

CHAPTER 6
SAM – JUST A BOY

Samrat Singh came from a house full of people. With three brothers and a sister, he had no clue what special treatment was. Everything was shared amongst five, and everything was divided into five. Be it love, time, attention, food, clothes, or money. Like it mostly happened in families with many kids, they too were each other's support when it came to anything outside the house, but inside, it was the survival of the fittest. And so, certain street smartness and the ability to deal with different mental setups got into the system. His father was conservative and a stickler for discipline. Guess he knew that with four boys, the best and easiest way was to chalk out a line of conduct beforehand and close the doors for open discussion or personal opinions. He had been a young boy himself once. He knew the right brakes.

The good thing with many siblings is that they rarely feel exclusively victimized by parental torture and their lack of understanding towards children's colossal everyday snags. A growing child is in a constant state of wants. The only child has no one around to compare notes with, and there is never an emotional syllabus available for him to consult. Nor does he have any means of evaluating whether what he has been served in childhood is fantastic, good, average or horrible. Siblings sometimes look at each other and wipe away complaints. So though, there could have been a slight murmur here and there, mostly amongst them, there was never so much of an open rebellious challenge that was thrown toward the parents. And toward the father even less, if not never.

Samrat's father was a successful surgeon, so the money was plenty, and his presence in the house was scarce. An early start of the day went on till late in the night. For a house full of siblings and a mother at their service, it was a dream house, barring the night when the pressure was felt a little. But children made their routine around the presence and decided that early to bed worked out for all concerned parties. Their father was too preoccupied and too tired and seldom had enough energy or interest to follow up on the kids, knowing his wife knew what she needed to do. If need be, she knew he was there to pull the strings. Money he provided plenty; love and care was the mother's responsibility, which she too provided plenty, and which in his mind was more than sufficient. His job was to instil the discipline and fear of failing, and he did that with great gusto.

Little fear was also the result of being exposed to the surgeon's knife and other creepy-looking tools that were revealed to them in their formative years. Once or twice, when things got out of hand with the tiny lot, the only option left in her mind was to use scare tactics. Their mother displayed the contents of their father's bag, with an imaginary frightening story of mischievous children being at the receiving end of it. That left a lingering dread in their psyche, and after a lot of consultation amongst themselves, the young ones concluded that if they wanted to survive, they had to toe the line.

It was a mystery to most how the Singh boys were so sorted. If the secret of the impactful bag were ever to be revealed, the bag would have been as big a hit as Molina's dolls. For different reasons altogether, but nevertheless as much in demand.

So, the household had a different vibe in the day and different at night. An early night meant early morning, and so to avoid running into a 'fresh from a good night's sleep and fully charged up for the day,' dad, two of the boys started the habit of going for a morning jog. One took to yoga and one to a cycle. All boys were busy with healthy routines approved by their father.

Some things begin in your life with an absolutely wrong intention and then take the shape of a blessing. What they call a blessing in disguise. It happened with the Singh boys, too. They got into the good habit of sleeping early, unlike boys of their age, who spent their nights in front of laptops and mobile phones surfing the internet or chatting, making them more energetic and focused than their sleep-deprived peers. Their morning cardio kept them fit and feeling good, and they realized the importance and benefits of physical exercise. It boosted their overall personality and confidence. All four Singh boys excelled in studies and extracurricular activities. Sam was one of the two who went jogging, and ever since, his steps refused to stay idle. He became a walker. A very keen walker.

Unfortunately, Sam stood last in the looks department of his family. An exceptionally good-looking lot with sparkling personalities, the other three boys could stand next to any Greek God and win. And his sister's looks were the kind to start a war. Sam could be called reasonably handsome but in any other surroundings. At home, he couldn't compete, nor could he go outside since all through his childhood, the boys moved in a pack. It was their mother's desire that the Singh boys display unanimity and brotherhood at all times. She didn't want her attention spread out in different directions if the boys were ever to venture out on their own. With an absentee husband, she had her hands full anyway. Thus, Sam was pushed into constant companionship with his siblings. The attention and affection the cuter ones got didn't do much for Sam's confidence, and he craved to be noticed. Childhood social neglect has diverse consequences in adults. He made him exploit it when he began getting it in later years. The competition had left his side, and he had the field all to himself, and he played on it and how.

He avoided hanging out with his brothers and devoted his time digging his nose in the books. Though he was an average student, repeating the same text gave him an edge over the smarter ones who evaded looking at it. He began scoring better, and soon, the swap felt like a boon. The eyes started darting towards him as he emerged as the brighter one, and soon, the magic of looks began fading. He had found his mantra. You can't fight with what nature made, but you can fight with what you can make with your nature. He set out to work on himself and promised to score wherever he could. But the desire to be desired by the opposite sex never left him, and the childhood neglect created a vacuum that never found its fill.

He was just about eleven years old when he first noticed a strange feeling that disturbed him whenever his younger sister's friend Vinisha visited their house. She stayed down the road, and both she and his sister Sameera found a safe haven in each other's houses. Their parents encouraged it as the girls thus stayed in the vicinity. Sam stayed around, too. First, to avoid getting ignored outside, but then soon because home front offered him an uninterrupted, free space to ogle at Vinisha. He didn't know why the day suddenly became better as soon as she entered. Sanjana was a protected sister and thus didn't develop any fangs, claws or horns. Her life was a dish served on a platter, and her skill set was restricted to devouring it. She would find Sam lurking around their dolldom on a regular basis, but she was too clueless to do anything about it. She was young too. So was Sam. He, just like Vinisha, is all he felt. It took him close to three years to know that she didn't.

One day, he found her with his elder brother Samay in the back alley, and he didn't like what he saw, not out of jealousy but out of concern. Vinisha was sitting on the stone edge of a tree, and from afar, it looked like she was crying profusely. Samay was looking the other way instead of looking into the matter. The scene looked heartless on his brother's account, and Vinisha seemed to be his victim. It was Sam's Vinisha, or so he thought. He gallantly marched towards them with the intention of saving his Vinisha from the villain that his brother appeared to be.

He shouldn't have. If he had turned away that day, maybe the Sam we saw today wouldn't have happened. Upon reaching, he heard Samay scornfully lashing at Vinisha with disinterest. He didn't try to find out the reason. He straightaway extended his hand and tried to pull Vinisha up. She shrugged his hand and resisted. He tried again, and when he failed, he sat down next to her. In that very fraction, he felt the dynamics changing from her side. She was unusually stiff and rigid and shifted herself away from him. It didn't look like she needed his comforting company. Confused, he sat there wondering how to rescue her when his brother bent down and gave his final warning.

"You will go first thing tomorrow and confess to Kavi that you were behind all those disgusting love letters that you claimed that I have been sending to you. You will make sure that Kavi knows the truth and more so believes it. If I lose Kavi because of you, you will find yourself crying like this for the rest of your life. There are handwriting experts, if you don't know. It will take me no time to prove your dirty tricks and put it on display." He paused to grasp his breath and then shot back, "I am giving you one chance to right your wrongdoings, all because you are Sameera's best friend. But if you even look in my direction, I will make sure your masterpieces are in every hand around town." Samay straightened himself, gave a pitiful glance at Sam and walked away.

Sam was still processing the devastating details and had yet to reach the verdict when he heard a feeble, "But I love you, Samay. I love you so much."

A crushed Sam got up from there with a very distorted version of what love was.

***

CHAPTER 7
WHERE IT ALL BEGAN

She was sixteen years old, riding a bicycle with Urvi, when she had the life-altering run-in with Sam. Trying to race up each other, Molina's bicycle wheel knocked a large rock on the side of the road, and she landed face down on the ground. Urvi, in her competitive spirit, went on ahead vigorously pedalling her cycle. Looking back was not an option, as she feared that one glance might cost her her victory.

As Urvi was cycling towards an exhilarating win with all her might, her injured friend was lying somewhere far behind. Molina lay all alone, bleeding profusely on a deserted road. It was such a pitiful sight that Sam couldn't help but stop to check on the girl. He had taken to the quiet street to clear his head after an ugly altercation with a friend over a girl. But that could wait.

For a twenty-year-old Sam, this was a chance to prove his responsibility as a young man. There was no question of not coming to the rescue of a damsel in distress. He bent down on his knees to check the physical damage, and his eyes rested on the pool of blood collected near the girl's head. He knew he couldn't waste any time. He picked her up in his arms and started marching towards the main road. He was trying to make a quick decision in his head as to where to go. He would have to turn into the main road to find the nearest doctor or clinic, and he gallantly kept walking the long stretch of the lonely road.

For Molina, he was a godsend. Lying there by the road, she was in shock. Her heart was pounding with fear of not being found, and her whole body felt like it had broken into pieces. The pain was slowly invading her, and she was feeling helpless like never before.

And then, as strong arms lifted her, in an instant, she felt safe. As she was being taken, God knows where, she felt a kind of sweet pleasure slowly overpowering the shooting pain, and suddenly, it was not all that bad. She was severely injured, with blood still oozing out of her head. To stay conscious was proving to be a struggle, but she wanted him to keep going with her in his arms. Her heart started praying that where he was taking her was miles away, so she could stay in the moment forever.

Sam hadn't even brought his phone along. So, all he could do under the circumstances was to carry the girl and walk. But then he was a walker, not a weight lifter. Carrying someone for long was not what he was used to. Though the silken hair falling over his arms was sending a sweet sensation to his being and holding a heart so close to his own heart was proving to be somewhat intoxicating, to keep going further was becoming a challenge. The discomfort was turning into agony, and he hoped someone would pass by. Anyone, as long as he got some help. Between both his and her prayers, so far, only Molina's were being answered after walking quite a bit of a distance and almost on the verge of giving up. He had thought of himself as the guy from the movies, carrying a girl to the hospital in his arms in slow motion and coming out looking like a macho saviour. Sam thought he could do it. It looked so easy in the movies. With his fitness and stamina, Sam was supposed to be that hero. But he was done trying to be one. Damn the movies.

He needed to put the girl down, and he was about to do so when he heard the sound of a bicycle bell. He turned to look and saw another girl of the same age approaching with full vigour. It was Urvi who had come in search of her missing friend. Seeing Urvi in sight immediately lessened his pain. And though he didn't realize it, his heroism partially returned. He lifted Molina back up so as not to lose the opportunity to be mentioned in future folklore for his selfless bravery.

Urvi hurriedly got down from the still moving cycle, clearly aware that her friend was in peril. Shock, horror, guilt was written all over her being. Without wasting a minute, she took out her phone and called her father. He was needed there faster than the wind was all she said.

"What the hell has happened? What have you done to her? Why is she covered in so much blood? Who are you, and where are you taking her?"

Panting and shaking, she went on throwing one question after another, not giving Sam a chance to reply.

"He is helping me," Molina's feeble voice managed in the hope of calming her panic-stricken friend. But to no avail.

"Hello, I am talking to you. Why are you standing here like a statue, and why are you holding her like a trophy? Don't you think you should have taken her to the hospital? Did you call for any help? Of course not. Your dumb face says you haven't. And I don't see any magic wand here… So? What are you waiting for?" she fumed, hiding the increasing self-blame behind the aggression.

Molina, too weak to try another attempt, helplessly let Sam get attacked.

Finding a chance between a pause for breath by Urvi, Sam stuttered,

I… I… I don't have a phone."

The ranting stopped, and understanding and appreciation replaced it.

"Oh, okay," is all that she could utter.

Finding the opportunity to put across to Urvi that he did his best, he said,

"All I could do was carry her, hoping for any kind of help. She fell right at the beginning of the turn. Been walking all this distance and had halted as my arms are unable to hold her any longer."

Urvi nodded.

"Whom did you call?" Without wasting a second, he added. "How long before they are here?"

"My dad. I called my dad."

"Is he coming? How far is he?" Getting no further information about the help on the way, his urgency made him restless.

Before Urvi could answer, they both heard the siren of an ambulance and turned to see that it was speeding fast toward them. A few more seconds later, Sam knew he had made it. Finally, his painful journey had come to an end, and Molina was put on the spread-out stretcher in front of them. In between the hectic transfer into the ambulance, one attendant came forward to ask who was accompanying the injured. Urvi thought for a moment and told Sam to go with them. He was her saviour, and he should see it through as she needed to wait for her dad.

She thought it best to call him again. With Molina safely in the ambulance, she felt free enough to call. He said he was a minute away. Knowing her dad, she wished he really was a minute away, as living with him, she knew his punctuality was questionable.

"Can you please come fast?" And to make it more impactful added, "They have taken her to the hospital, and I am standing alone on the road waiting for you."

Though the ambulance had still not left, she saw no harm in lying a little herself to her forever-lying dad.

As they prepared to leave with Molina, she told them to carry on and that she was being picked soon.

As the taillights were moving away, she saw two headlights moving towards her.

Her dad had arrived. She ran and sat in the car. She burst out crying. Overwhelming helplessness often becomes worse in the presence of your parents. The strength and courage that you pull together in their absence to cope with difficulties just leave your grip. And you just want to hand over all of the collected anguish to them to handle. You know they will take over. There was no use asking the howling girl anything, so the father silently drove to the hospital.

At the hospital, Molina's parents and Urvi's mom were already waiting. It took the doctor forty-five minutes to come out and give them an update.

"Molina is a bit critical as a lot of blood has been lost, and she still has to regain consciousness. They will need to keep her in there for a few days till the time her blood is in sufficient volume. And though she is not really in any danger, a hairline fracture will keep her in bed for a few weeks. It's just a bit of a wait till she is good as new," the doc explained with both caution and assurance. "I am glad you guys brought her in the nick of time, as any further delay would have definitely been fatal," he added and turned to attend to his patient.

If he had not added the last bit, perhaps the story of Molina and Sam's life would have been different. 'It would have been fatal' hung in the air for the group present there. A life was saved. And suddenly, all eyes turned to Sam.

Sam, on his part, was in a state of confusion. Whether he was to be blamed for the delay that resulted in so much blood loss, or would he be patted on his back for caring enough to have stopped and rescued her? He decided to go with the latter. He did save a life, after all. Didn't the doctor just say that? And so, he thought it best to continue waiting with the family in the hope that he would be heaped with praises.

He didn't have to wait long. While he was conflicting with his emotions, all eyes had already turned on him.

With the doctor gone, the waiting crew began the expected chatter. What exactly happened? How did Sam come to the scene? Where was Urvi and most importantly, how did Sam manage to carry Molina in his arms for such a long distance?

With Molina in the safe care of the doctor and the hospital, the focus shifted to the man of the moment. The elders were not only thanking him but also counting his attributes, which he himself never realized he possessed.

"Who stops to help anyone nowadays," said Urvi's mom.

"And that, too, someone lying on the road bleeding?"

Molina's father picked up the conversation. "Most would run away fearing the police."

"Absolutely. And imagine a young boy at that? What courage and what concern."

To make the gratitude and admiration look more impactful, Molina's father stepped closer to Sam and put his arm around him.

"You have no idea about your gallant act, do you? You are standing here so unassuming and modest, as if this is what your everyday looks like. You have saved a life, my daughter's life," he said with eyes at the brink of welling up.

"You know I will forever be in your debt. If I could ever be of any help to you, promise me you will not hesitate," her dad said, like most people do, under these kinds of circumstances.

Sam kept looking down, still getting used to this sudden shift of attention towards him and the outpour of praise. It was the first in his life, all so new. He was always amongst the crowd. With five siblings leading pretty much identical lives, they were praised or punished in no manner different. Standing alone holding a trophy was not the experience he or any one of them ever had.

That day's incident was going to change all that.

Molina's dad said, "Your father will be so proud of you when he hears about your bravery." When he heard the words, it dawned upon him that there was an advantage attached to the whole incident. That he might have just got an exclusive pass to different kind of stardom. He decided to sound like it was no big a deal to make it look more heroic.

"I am sure anyone would have done the same in my place," he said softly, still looking down.

Urvi's dad had meanwhile gone to fetch some refreshments, and when he returned with a full bag, Sam noticed he was the first one to be offered snacks and cola. It was almost dinnertime, and he definitely was hungry. Soon, he would be sleepy, too. But then, he was enjoying the attention too much to ask for their leave. He wasn't needed there, but he stayed put till an unsympathetic nurse arrived and told them that they all would have to leave, save one, who would be staying with the patient.

Barring Molina's mother, the rest began departing after hugging her and spouting reassurances that everything would be alright.

CHAPTER 8
THE AFTERMATH

Sam, still learning the ways of the world, still at the threshold of emotional calculation, waited to follow everyone out yet didn't indulge in any further participation. Once outside, phone numbers were exchanged and byes were said. It looked like his day had come to an end. And it did. He was a walker and he went back home walking. Nothing could lure him away from walking.

The next day was another story. The neighbourhood was abuzz with the tales of the previous night, and a couple of early morning calls to Sam's house-made sure his favourite breakfast was on the table coupled with a 'love you and proud of you' note signed by his already 'left for work' dad. Mom's grin was definitely wider, warmer, and authentic, unlike the habitual one she was accustomed to flashing at every child who met her eyes. Two of his brothers, Samman and Samay, both older than him, had a little bit of suspicion in their eyes as if anticipating a change in his attitude. He wasn't sure how, but they seemed threatened. Although he got a tight hug and a well done from both of them, which was not the practice among themselves, as they lived under the same roof. He felt he was going to be watched for some time.

It normally happens that when things change for the better for someone, people around him start changing towards him, even before he realizes that things have changed for him. Some people change for the better, some for the worse. In Sam's house, the divide happened. For the elder lot, he had marched past them. The younger ones, his sister Sameera and the youngest brother Samrajya, on the other hand, found an opportunity to flash his name around and shine in the spotlight of a famous brother. All in all, life was good.

During the day, he thought a lot about the night and the new acquaintances and wondered what must be happening with them. He decided he would call Urvi later and inquire about Molina. Somehow, he liked the name Molina. Rare name that could fit into any country and any religion. He should call up and ask after the family, too. The father looked very gentle and simple. What would it be like to have him as a father, he wondered, having a tough and rigid one of his own?

Before he could, Urvi called him on his cell. The girl is sharp, he thought as he answered. She must have memorized his cell number as he was giving it to Molina's father. He clearly remembered not giving it to her.

"Hey, superman," she said cheerfully, "Ready with your cape?"

"Huh, what?" he mumbled, "Who?"

"Your angel on the bicycle," she laughed, half amused and half sarcastic.

"Oh, yes, of course. Of course. That you certainly are," he said something out loud that he had been saying to himself all along. If it wasn't for her, Sam wouldn't have been able to reach the hospital in time. The crown deserves to be on both their heads.

"So, treat?" Urvi took her chance, "Shouldn't you treat the angel?"

"Of course, I should." He, too, went along.

"But shouldn't you, too? After all, I saved your best friend."

After pausing for a moment, Urvi said, "If you put it this way, then sure, you deserve more. Meet me in the hospital cafeteria. 5:30? We will first check in on Mols followed by the treat."

"Perfect. I meant to visit myself. We have to see it through, right?"

Suited him fine, he thought.

"Absolutely. No respite before that. See ya."

It was in the cafeteria that they clicked their coffee mocha glasses and celebrated their small victory. It was the first time both of them recognized the feeling of fulfilment in helping and being of use. Celebrations were definitely in order.

They had a long chat, and would often speak to each other after that. And by the time Molina got discharged to go home, Urvi and Sam had become good friends and knew few of each other's friends too. The three families also initially got to know a little bit about each other. But it was the much-awaited dinner invitation for Sam that finally got them together. A day was decided and invitations were sent to both Sam's and Urvi's families.

***

While the preparations for dinner were taking place, Molina was trying to improve her appearance and gait. She thought she would be the next topic of discussion among Sam's family, which she heard was large compared to hers. Sam was still a mystery boy for her, and though Urvi, in her exaggerated versions, had told her a lot about him, she still had to get to know him herself. She was still young enough to have any strong romantic feelings, yet she was old enough to develop a crush. And she had begun to, thanks to Urvi.

The day arrived, and the three families assimilated. After the initial formalities, everybody started warming up to each other, and the simplicity of the hosts made it easier. Though there was financial disparity between Molina's and the other two families, it didn't hinder the exchange of warmth and appreciation. For the most part, Sam and his family were being discussed for being the best at everything, having a prolific and accomplished surgeon for a father, the mother a dignified lady of the house and such intelligent, well-brought-up, kind and caring children. The credit went to the parents when a kid triumphed, and Sam's father happily not only received the compliments but secretly believed in them, too.

In all of this, somewhere Molina was forgotten. Not even mentioned. There was not even a fleeting spotlight on her. There was nothing about her that was required to be discussed. All she did was fall over a stone while cycling. That happens with children every other day. But for her, she was the cause of all that followed. She was the opening scene and she should be in the entire movie. But that was not to be.

Highly dejected and disillusioned, she withdrew into her room for a bit in the hope that she would be missed and soon would be called upon. Then there'd be a mention of her dolls. Oh, her dolls. They were sure to leave an impression. They always did. Looking out the window of her room, she was playing in her mind on how to introduce her story into the conversation when she saw figures coming out in the dark from under her window. They were leaving! The guests were leaving. No one had looked for her. Not Sam, not her parents. Not even her friend Urvi.

A strange king of determination found a place in her head. For the first time in her life, she realized she didn't like being overlooked. Maybe it was her years of being at the forefront because of her artistic success that made her accustomed to being spoken about all the time, or maybe her newly discovered attraction towards a boy was seeking attention. Whatever it was, it didn't go down well with her; that night, she hadn't existed at all. It was as if she blended into the background, and nobody was able to see her. Gone were the days when she used to blend into the background. She was at the forefront, and she intended to stay there.

She got up the next morning, bright as a daisy. She had a lot of work to do. The shy little girl had a lot of work to do on herself. She thought and decided against involving Urvi in her plot. She would have to do it herself. Her self-respect raised its little head. Another first for her. She began her metamorphosis. She already had a lot going on in her favour in terms of achievements. She just needed window dressing to be better. She upped her dressing game. She was creative, so she used her aesthetics to create her own style. She ate right, went running, and paid attention to her skin and hair. She developed a swagger, and her head was lifted with confidence. Each day was an improvement, and soon, all eyes were on her. From the girl who fell down, she became the girl who rose. Rose to stardom.

By this time, she was eighteen years old. Though she had met Sam here and there as Urvi and he were now friends, she avoided him as she felt she needed more time to work on herself. He was on her mind constantly as he was the only boy who had come anywhere near her. But she was not one to chase, and she was willing to wait to be chased. Sam, on his part, was getting more and more intimidated by her physical transformation and increasing popularity. She was also on his mind, and in spite of having access to her best friend and occasionally to her folks, he never tried to befriend her in that manner. So, years passed with both of them at the other end of the spectrum.

Distance may make the hearts grow fonder, but time can also slowly fade everything away – memories, emotions, and feelings. And if it's a teenage crush, even more so. In Molina's case, too, it began to dwindle. She was inviting a lot of attention, which girls of that age usually do. But she was being adulated and how. In two years' time, Sam's good deed also lost most of its sheen. The equilibrium was in her favour now, and her desire to prove a point was diminishing.

Molina got the attention she worked towards, but realized she didn't care about the source of any. The line up of lanky directionless boys didn't do anything for her. She didn't like any of them. She didn't need any one of them. Sam was also almost forgotten as being few years her senior, their paths rarely crossed. It seemed the entire Sam saga happened in her life to make her learn and unlearn a few things.

In life, when you get what you desperately want, even after a long and hard wait, the euphoria is only short-lived.

You may want something today that you may not want later.

That's when she learned the second lesson of her life.

***

CHAPTER 9
DESTINY PAUSED

The three years that she gave to her teenage frivolousness and the outcome of it made her a wee bit more mature than girls of her age. While they were discovering boys, she was discovering herself. Done with all the frills, she dived into academics with a bang. Her life revolved around her studies. She knew she wasn't very bright, but she was ready to work hard. She was unambitious, but she needed to earn a living. And though her toy-art was still getting her steady income, it wasn't enough to fulfil the dreams she had for her parents. She had to make more money. A brief chat with the career counsellor gave her the best possible option. She was fit to be an interior designer. Her aptitude for all things creative, her artistic imagination and her aesthetics were just the right mix required for success in that field.

And at twenty-two, she was a qualified interior designer.

She fared well at her degree; she was hard working and she was sincere. She got a good recommendation from her professors and got selected from the campus itself. She was offered an internship with a very reputable architecture firm.

And that's where she met Sam again.

She ran into him while visiting a sight for her immediate boss. She didn't recognize him at first. He had a stubble and a ponytail, and he had muscled up. Plus, she was not paying much attention. She was on the job, and that's where her mind was. It was Sam who, after studying her for a while, said, "Molina, right? Are you Molina? From North Avenue Road?"

It was Molina's turn to study the face that seemed to know her. Of course, she knew him. But she couldn't recall from where.

"I am so sorry. I know your face is so familiar but I am not being able to recollect where we met."

After struggling for a bit, she apologized.

"Not your fault, really," Sam smiled. "You were half unconscious when we met the first time." He chuckled. "And we've not really met much after that. Anyway, it was a long time ago. So… yaa... I guess you can be forgiven."

Though a little disappointed, Sam made light of the matter.

"Oh... of course. You are Sam. How stupid of me."

Molina felt like beating herself. No matter how her younger self had taken the Sam episode as a competition and challenge, her now mature self was full of gratitude and remorse – gratitude for saving her life and remorse for not acknowledging it back then.

"How can I ever forget you? I owe you my life. Oh God. You must think of me as so ungrateful. But truth is… you know... a new job. Nervous. Just been preoccupied is all…" she tried to sound as apologetic as she felt.

"I get it… I totally get it... I, too, have been there… I know." He smiled. "I know the anxiety and pressure of an unfamiliar playground."

He tried to make her feel at ease.

"You will feel like a pro in no time. Trust me," he said encouragingly and changed the topic. "How have you been? Clearly, it is very good on the work front, as far as I can see. But otherwise, I hope all is well. Are Mom and Dad good? Would love to see them sometime. I have such good memories of them."

"Mom and Dad are fine. You must come to visit them whenever you can. You know they are immensely fond of you."

"I know. I should have kept in touch with them. And, of course, you."

There. He had said it. He said it and realized that years of waiting had finally formed words and came out so naturally and so effortlessly. No preparation and no rehearsal would have achieved the effect of the ease with which it came out. And boy, was he glad!

"Ya... We should have. But I guess at that age, we had too many roads ahead of us to know which one to take and which one to leave." She gave it a philosophical touch.

They were at Sam's boss's new office space, where Molina's firm was assigned to do the interiors. It was to be his corporate law firm's new office, and the instructions gave an international feel to it. He showed her around the place while she took photos. As she was busy measuring the requirements for furniture placements, he ordered coffee and waited for her to finish. By the time the coffee arrived, she was done taking all the details. They sat down on the windowsill of the bare office and caught up on the last few years while drinking their coffee.

The project took eight months to complete, giving both of them ample time and opportunity to not only learn about each other but also get accustomed to each other. The memory of Molina's popularity was fresh in Sam's mind, and he was hell-bent on going the extra mile now that he had the chance. He went on a mission to woo her with single-minded dedication. Initially, Molina was a hard nut to crack, as too much attention too early in life made her immune to any kind of flattery or adulation. Sam soon understood that all he needed to do was be real and treat her just like everybody else. He just needed to be himself and let her be herself. He consciously never mentioned her exceptional beauty and her charismatic persona. It helped as Molina, without realizing it, was freed from the unnecessary stress of minding her appearance. He only spoke about her artistry and her insight, her simplicity and her honesty, her maturity and her ethics.

He did another wise and favourable thing. He gave her space. He never demanded attention, never fought for more of her time. He made sure she attended to all her tasks and duties and readily put himself second to it all. There were seldom any disagreements and often unspoken understanding. Neither tried to be difficult, and neither tried to be assertive. It was the camaraderie of equals, and it suited them both. They found that they were in perfect sync together, whether it was work-related or outside of work. All this came as a relief to Molina. He became her official pick-up and drop guy, her regular meal partner, and her weekend movie buddy and slowly and gradually, he seeped into her system. It was she who now reached out to the phone to call him whenever she found time. She started running a marathon every time her phone or doorbell rang. She thought of him when he was not with her, and she thought of no other when he was with her. And one fine day, she woke up knowing that she had fallen in love. She had fallen in love with Sam.

But she was in no hurry to tell him. She decided to wait and test her feelings. Sam dropped hints about what she meant to him, but she needed to hear the declaration. She needed to hear those three golden words, which are meant to change the course of one's life. It was when she got a job revamping an old palace into a hotel somewhere in the deserts of Rajasthan that Sam's heart sank with blues. He didn't waste any time, and the next night, he arranged a romantic setting by the same windowsill of his now fully furnished office and went down on his knees.

It was an immediate 'yes' from Molina.

***

Three years passed before they gave marriage a thought. It was a spoken promise that they made to each other, that lie and deceit would not find a place between them. That was Molina's primary and only condition. She would not be lied to and her trust would not be betrayed. They promised each other and like all lovers, they believed each other. Looking forward to a rosy life ahead, they set a wedding date.

But luckily for Molina and Sam, the wedding stayed on the logical path. And that too out of choice because in Sam's case, his was to be the third wedding in his family. There were two more to go, so the excitement levels were terribly low. They were just a year or so apart, so they were still recovering from the previous ones. They voted for a simple one.

Molina's parents would have wanted the world at her feet, as she was their only daughter, and this was their only opportunity to have a real celebration for her, but money was a restraint. They could have managed with a reasonably plush affair, what with Molina's years of steady earnings from her handicrafts work along with a lucrative job. But Molina felt wrong to rob her parents of their financial security. In her parents' eyes, it was her money, but her calculation went differently. Whatever she was today was the result of their labour and sacrifices, and they were the rightful shareholders of the final produce. Everything in their life was split three ways. No arguing there.

Preparations went reasonably smoothly and the disagreements, if any, were minor and got resolved quickly. All were on the same page. The guest list was drawn, and the number of guests was divided into equal numbers for both sides since the expenditure was also to be divided equally.

There was one name which appeared on both lists and was noticed by both sides yet not removed from either. It was Urvi's name.

***

Urvi. Yes, the only common link between them. The only one who knew them as closely as they knew each other. Urvi had got accustomed to living in Molina's shadows, and it didn't seem to arouse any kind of jealousy or insecurity. Maybe when Molina picked up speed in her popularity, they had been little girls, and at that age, the sharing of pain and pleasure was generally very real and genuine. The intensity of love and devotion was strong and single-minded. Molina's time and affection were only reserved for Urvi. That every eye was on Molina was definitely an added bonus. It's a very heady feeling to be exclusively wanted by someone who is wanted by everyone.

So, Urvi stayed. Stayed with her friend. Stayed by her side through everything.

Their small-scale venture had picked up reasonably well. They added a lot of other useful pieces created from eco-friendly and recycled materials, which got them a lot of applause and very distinct elite-class patrons. An NGO got involved, and a large number of underprivileged women were hired and trained. The passion had also become a cause, and it started feeling like they were shouldering a responsibility. Molina would drift a bit whenever she had needed time for her studies in the past, and now, when the workload increased, they had been managing it with flair, along with all their accompanying commitments.

For Urvi that was it. She carried it several notches up with her hard work and Molina was sure whatever she would do, Urvi was to stay on board. From then on, the friendship of the heart joined friendship of the mind and matter.

They were inseparable, and Urvi knew each and every page of Molina's love story and vice versa. And like all best friends, it was not unusual for them to voice their displeasure or reservations about each other's choices and decisions. Urvi was forever giving up on boys that Molina didn't approve of. She had a hawk's eye as far as her friend's interests were concerned. Urvi trusted her judgment and never once questioned her; forget about even offering counterarguments. It was an unwritten rule. They were there for each other the way no one else was. And the rule was never broken. Not until....

***

CHAPTER 10
THE PROPOSAL

When Sam dropped her home after proposing to her that night, the first thing Molina did was call Urvi. She had not even entered the house and was fidgeting with the handle of the gate, not ready to face her parents till she heard her bestie's screams of joy. Urvi took some time to pick up the phone. It was not her fault, as it was 3:30 at night, and she had been asleep for over three hours. Deep sleep takes away the roughness of the day gone by and spreads a cast of such soothing refuge that the effect is almost intoxicating. And to be woken up from that, especially at odd hours, is something not easily pardonable.

Urvi picked up the phone and sounded, at first annoyed, very annoyed. But when she heard her friend's out of breath, 'hey' she became a little worried.

"Mols, what happened? You okay," she whispered, shaking off her sleep. "What time is it?"

Was it late in the night, or had she overslept, and dawn had already descended? She tried to rub her eyes to see if she could spot the time on her phone. Her father had made sure there was no bedside switch in the children's room. He was of the opinion that kids should walk up to everything and that easy access made them lethargic.

Molina needed her friend wide awake, so she waited to break the news.

"It's late, like really late. And I am more than okay." She tried to calm her down.

"Then what are you doing calling at this hour?" Learning all was well with her, Urvi's irritation returned. "Whatever it is, I am sure it could have waited till a few hours."

She reached out for her comforter to pull it over herself and begged, "Please, Mol, not now. Promise I will call you soon as I get up." Her words were barely audible now, and Molina knew she wasn't listening to her any more. There were very few things that could lure or shake someone out of the lap of ultimate drunkenness. Urvi, too, refused to oblige, and after a feeble 'good night', she hung up.

There was no point calling again. Molina was okay and beyond that Urvi didn't care. Not at that hour.

Molina was right outside her own house, and her wish to break the news first to Urvi didn't come true. She began tiptoeing towards the main door. She would quietly enter and go to her room and wait for the morning to break. She knew her parents would probably be awake in bed. She rarely did late nights, and when she did, they were always in the know about her return. They were lenient, trusted her and let her make her own decisions. She was just required to keep them informed. That night was different. That night had gone by without her realizing where it had gone. She had forgotten to inform them, so she sneaked in.

Hearing no sound from them till she reached her room, she heaved a sigh of relief. Gently closing her bedroom door, she went straight to bed and lay down. Sleep was going to be elusive, she knew. Her mind was in overdrive, and she was amazed at its capacity to entertain so many different kinds of emotions, all at the same time. She was blissful, ecstatic, nervous, and anxious, yet she was restless, confused, scared, and numb. The most beautiful night of her life was also the most trying.

If only Urvi wasn't such a baby. If only she had held the phone a wee bit longer and given Molina a chance to justify the odd-hour call. Molina would have offloaded the night on Urvi and would have been unburdened now. If only Urvi wasn't such a baby.

She would now have to be in bed till her folks left for work, or else there would be a mention of the previous night, and she would have to divulge the details. She didn't want to do that early in the morning. Early mornings are rushed. She wanted a perfect setting to reveal the happiest news of all their lives. She wanted it to be like a well-written scene out of a movie. She stayed in bed till she heard the front door being opened and shut twice. Till she heard the fading sounds of familiar footsteps, she stayed put in bed. And then she sat up and began planning.

The previous night had taken her by surprise, and she was happy it did. Not one to get jittery or skittish, she knew that a little hint would also have spoiled it for her. Even slight knowledge of any upcoming occurrence builds up some kind of expectation. And it rarely outwits our imagination or our hope.

That's because, when it comes to our own lives, we can definitely write a better script than God can.

In most cases, at least.

***

Molina sat for a while in bed, going over the previous day. It was not yet sinking in, but the fervour was waning. The urgency to share was replaced with how and when to share. She wasn't expecting Urvi's apologetic call for shutting Molina out like that the previous night. She was sure Urvi would not have any memory of it at all.

And though she was upset about it, she realized now that she was glad it didn't go through her way. She doubted if Urvi would have lived up to Molina's imagined level of ecstasy in the state that she was. Nor could Molina have matched up to Urvi's zeal and zest if she were to be wide awake and absorbing all of it that late at night. Her entire self was exhausted and dazed with amazement and exhilaration. Bliss can numb you in a good way. The serenity of the night did her good. It composed her nerves and took care of the whim. She was back to being the ever-so-in-control Molina.

Since she decided she was in no hurry, she went about her morning like any other. There was a missed call from Sam, her brand-new fiancé, her so-far secret fiancé. She needed a cup of coffee before she returned the call. She had spent the night drifting in and out of sleep and was aware that she was still too groggy to perk up to that kind of chat. She made her coffee, sat by the kitchen window, took too many sips too quickly and picked up the phone to dial Sam.

She was ready now to re-live the night with him, this time in conversation.

As she unlocked her phone, Urvi's name flashed on the screen. An eager smile formed on her face.

"Hey!" Urvi chirped.

Molina waited.

"Done with your coffee? Good to go?" Urvi was doing what best friends do. Let you know that they can read you even when they can't see you.

"Mom has made waffles. Get you some for tea time?" she continued.

Is she luring me? Is she bribing me? Molina wondered. When did Urvi start taking her permission before making any decision, too, for something as minor as packing a waffle? From Urvi, there have only been orders. Orders, which left very little scope for a refusal. Mentally, Urvi always had more energy and verve. She could argue better, persuade more, and even cajole non-stop for what she wanted. And often succeeded, at least with Molina.

"You there? Mol? Hello?"

"Hmmm…" is all she chose to say. Wait a bit longer, is all she thought.

"I am halfway out of the door, Mol. Say fast. Shall I pack some for you?" Urvi was rushing. Rushing out and disconnecting the call.

She clearly had no recollection of the late-night call, so no discussion should be expected. With last night written off, it was to start afresh.

"Would have loved to, but I was thinking about a long, lingering lunch with you today." She didn't want drama anywhere other than right in front of her.

"Why lunch? Can't we do coffee?" Typical of Urvi. She tells you what, when, where.

"Fine. Coffee's good, too. Meet me at four. Costa?"

"But wait, why are we meeting?" She picked up on the unusual request. It was a weekday. These two committed girls never enjoyed the luxury of midweek breaks.

"You off today or what?" Something had to make sense to her.

"Something like that. See ya!" Molina put an end to the speculations and even though she heard Urvi's voice about to form some response, and hung up. She knew if she continued, Urvi would make her divulge everything there and then. The girl had a way with grilling.

She decided against calling Sam and instead went on to get ready. It was going to be memorable day.

'Love you my (a heart emoji) and (a phone emoji) later'

She messaged him and stepped into the shower.

There was a widespread grin plastered on her face as she showered. Everything made her smile. The bathroom was looking cleaner, prettier; the water was falling on her with unusual force and was soothing her like never before. She stepped out and stood in front of the mirror. As the fog from the steam of the hot shower was fading, her reflection in the mirror began to clear and she found herself facing the best, most beautiful version of herself.

There are few days that fill us with so much happiness that the long list of our desires, wishes, and wants is forgotten and that day feels enough; perfect with nothing more needed. It was that day for her, and she was pleased with the day.

She knew she was much before time as she reached Costa. Urvi was never on time. She entered and looked for a table somewhere far away in the corner. Urvi was going to be dramatically loud and lurid. She was still examining the huge room when a set of frantically swaying hands drew her attention. What? Urvi? A surge of affection filled her.

This girl sure knew how to love.

***

CHAPTER 11
GUILT AND REGRET

The table that Urvi occupied was right in the centre. So much for privacy, Molina chuckled. Urvi was already up and waiting. They hugged like they did every time they met. Urvi felt Molina hugged harder and longer and she reciprocated cheerily. There was good news there somewhere, she could sense.

"Come on, give it to me. Give it to me fast..."

Her antenna had picked up the signal, and now there was no stopping her.

"Give you what?" Molina tried to play a little.

"Oh, so we are playing? Are we now?"

This girl lives in my brain for sure, Molina thought.

"You mind sitting first? Please?" There were some heads already turned towards them and their eyes were evaluating the possibility of some action.

"Here," Urvi not only sat down but sat down slowly and soundlessly, mimicking looking scared. She folded her hands on the table, fluttered her eyes and said, "This okay, miss?"

Molina couldn't hold back her laughter. She was so lucky to have this madcap in her life, she told herself. She leaned forward, took Urvi's hand into hers, and guided them to the ring on her finger. And waited.

There were no words spoken. None were needed.

Urvi's eyes dropped to the object that was being felt by her hands, and they froze. She froze. She was looking at an engagement ring on the fingers of her best friend. This was the most long-awaited moment of their lives. This was the day of the culmination of their years of planned and unplanned liaisons, gruelling screening for the right guy, fearful uncertainties, and multiple challenges to overcome puerile heartbreaks. This was the day when the train of your love life stopped at your desired destination; you got down there and made your home.

Seeing Urvi's eyes transfixed on her ring, Molina beamed.

"Hey!" she nudged. "Why do you look so stunned? We knew it was coming. Right? You knew," she said with a certain certainty.

Of course, Urvi was the only one to have a complete account of her day-to-day life. She couldn't not know.

"Of course, it took me kinda by surprise, too, you know. And since it was planned with so much perfection, without me having any inkling whatsoever."

She paused to gasp.

"And oh my god, was I beyond floored." Words began flowing like a river now that her barrage was broken. "Sam had so beautifully adorned the window where we first hung out together. Remember when I met him after ages? Remember I told you we sat on that uncomfortable windowsill for over an hour, chatting away, and when we finally stood up, our bums were tearing with pain? Same window," she gushed.

"Here." She took out her phone and started searching for the night's video recording. "See," she thrust her phone into Urvi's face. And that's when she noticed.

Urvi's eyes were elsewhere, her mind was elsewhere, and she herself was elsewhere.

Her friend had not spoken a word since the time the ring was flashed before her. She had not reacted; she had not even moved.

Suddenly, a look of concern replaced the cheerful face.

"What is it, my darling? All okay? You okay?" She sounded worried. She was worried. "You are so quiet. Why are you quiet? This isn't my Urvi. What's going on?"

"Oh, no, nothing. Nothing, sweetheart." Urvi tried to collect herself. Indeed, she had drifted. And she herself wasn't sure where.

"Don't lie!" Molina seemed to have forgotten about her own jubilation. All that mattered to her now was Urvi.

"Something is bothering you. I can tell. I can always tell. You know that, right? So please, no lying here. Come on."

There was so much urgency, concern, and worry in her voice that Urvi couldn't help but feel a strange kind of benevolence towards her.

This one is a pure, beautiful, simple soul. Her purity needs to be shielded. Her simplicity needs to be protected. Lips need to be sealed. Truth needs to be concealed. And hope only hope needs to be fostered.

Gathering whatever little acting abilities she had, Urvi widened her smile with all the beauty of a rainbow. Masking her distress, fear and misgivings, she got up,

"Up, up, up… Come on... get yourself up..." She put all her efforts into sounding chirpy.

"You don't break the best news of your life sitting across like an interviewer."

As she said it, it hit her that she didn't say 'our lives'. It was always we, us, ours for them. She hoped Molina didn't notice. But this one was far from 'their' best news. This one time, it might end up being the opposite of that for both of them.

"You gotta give me the best hug there is and help this amazing, amazing feeling sink in," she said with the fakest smile and found herself astonished at her own performance.

***

She could have saved her friend from this pain. She could have if she had had the courage to tell Molina the truth. The truth about Sam. About his philandering ways. She had heard about his repute as a flirt when she got to know him as a teenager. She was too young to make any sense of it, and he was a young man too. That is the age when all boys eye all girls. Plus, loads of false rumours and stories float around the campus. Some are true, but some are born out of envy, jealousy or a simple lack of similar opportunities. Also, most kids were at the receiving end over something or the other and preferred to believe what suited them. Urvi didn't believe any of the nonsense she got to hear about Sam. He was her friend, and he treated her like a buddy. There was no uncomfortable experience or suggestive behaviour that could leave her suspicious. He was sweet, fun, caring and clean. And that's how it stayed between them.

But then he walked into Molina's life back again. Urvi was on and off in touch with him. But she knew about his life, more on the society scene, as she would catch glimpses of it through social media. There were plenty of girls rotating in quick succession, and it was on reckless display. But then, he was single, and he was allowed to play the field. So, she didn't pay any heed.

Till Molina mentioned her dating him, even when Molina met him again for work, and they became friends, Urvi wasn't alarmed as she never expected them to ever end up together. They were two entirely different people with little or nothing in common. There was no future together for these two, as far as she was concerned.

Maybe if she hadn't been so sure, she would have alerted her friend right at the beginning. But she didn't, and she couldn't when things started getting serious between them. She silently prayed that Sam had truly fallen in love with her friend and that that was the end of his Casanova days. And Sam's love and devotion to Molina kept her hopes up. He had proved to be a dream boyfriend, and Urvi could see that he sincerely cared for Molina. She hoped he had put his wild days behind him. His social media posts were few and far between and were mostly either related to work or occasional celebratory photos with Molina. There was no other way to know much about him, and from the look of it, he seemed clean and new. Urvi's worries were, to a certain extent, put to rest.

It was over a year and some months later that Urvi got a whiff of Sam's deception. She and Molina were in the process of starting their NGO for underprivileged, uneducated single mothers. Their intent was to make them self-sufficient by giving them employment at their, by now, flourishing handicraft business. They were approaching possible donors to collect funds from companies which had separate quotas for CSR. On one such visit, Urvi had a run-in with Sam. The owner's daughter was looking after the CSR department, and Urvi was there to see her. A young girl straight out of college had given her the appointment for an early evening meet. She reached well in time but was asked to wait. Not making much of it, she sat down and picked up a glossy fashion magazine amongst the many lying on the table in front of her. The ideal treat to kill time, there was nothing in there that took your attention away from your surroundings, and so, while waiting and wondering at the extent of high life out there in the world, she felt she heard some weird sounds of heavy breathing and panting, coming from the room behind her. She was sitting right outside, and the wall was touching her back. When it started getting louder and faster with some addition of moaning and groaning, she knew some action was taking place inside. Soon, she could feel the movement and hear the quaking. There was nothing left to the imagination, and she smiled to herself. Reckless, defiant youth. So good to not care, she thought. She looked around and caught the eyes of the receptionist. She quickly averted them as if taking the blame for her boss. Urvi tried to give a reassuring smile to convey that it was no big deal, but she got the impression that it was something that was not approved by that side.

Finally, the door opened, and just to save her prospective benefactor from any kind of embarrassment, Urvi hastily put her headphones on and dug her nose deep into the magazine. She didn't need to do that. The loved-up duo, still reeling under the spell of each other, couldn't have been more oblivious. She would have kept her head buried if it wasn't for the familiar voice and the laugh that followed it. She heard it yet didn't believe it, and this state of denial made her peep through the side of her pages. There he was, in all his potent glory, seducing one woman out of her clothes while stripping another one of her trust.

It was Sam all right. And he had just made her worst fears come true.

She had to catch him in the act. He had to know that she knew. That Molina would now know. And that it was game over for him.

"Sam?"

She stood up and called out to him. He turned to look and stopped in his tracks. The playboy of a few minutes back was transformed into a silly pulp of a man whose juice was drawn out, and all that remained was the limp mash.

"Was that really you in there?"

She threw the question at him, but it was addressed more at her own disbelieving self. Wasn't that Molina's Sam? Isn't he the guy who has been professing his undying love for her? Wasn't he the guy who had been promising her the world and every happiness that there was to have? Of course, he was that guy. He was that Sam. But what was he doing there? What was he doing with the woman? And what was he doing with this woman in there?

"Wow, look at you. You look all washed out, like someone has just run you through a washer. Dirty linen, too, got washed, I hope?" There was no way he was getting out of here unscathed. She would ruin it for him, right there, right then. She wanted to spew venom in the hope that it would spread all over his self-esteem and his self-worth, killing it forever and making him powerless to cheat further. She had to try.

"Truth be told, I never ever in my wildest dream thought I would ever be so unhappy to see you. It's really excruciatingly painfully unhappy to see you. I know the feelings are mutual. For entirely different reasons though, but mutual."

She lifted her brow in a manner of what say? Then, turning towards the clueless bystander, she said, "This guy here, this one who just banged you, is a self-confessed, overtly persuasive lover of my best friend. I am a full-time witness to his pretentious sham of a love life."

She stepped back, gave her a good look and warned, "Don't know how all this pans out in your world, but in mine and my friend's, it's out of bounds. You may continue if you wish to, but trust me, this guy here will regret this day. And you will, too, if this guy ever steps in here again. Fuck your donation and fuck your support. For us, just a strong, steady backbone is enough to stand on our own. You will not find us bending that for any amount. And yes, you might need a new legal hand. This one has just put in his papers. And here is the stamp."

Saying that she turned to Sam, swung her right hand back and brought it with such force that when it landed on Sam's face, it shook him off his feet. He staggered towards the girl, who, in a reflex, quickly shoved him off herself, and he landed on his back, with his face smeared with horror and anger.

"It's just the beginning," she said coolly and walked out.

***

CHAPTER 12
THE RED FLAG

And after years, she now regretted not bringing that to Molina's knowledge.

She would have. She was going to. In fact, she had made up her mind that she would not let Molina entertain Sam, even for an explanation or an apology. It was a clear case of betrayal, and there was no other way to look at it. He was out. He had to be.

But Sam was on his feet in no time and ran out to follow her. He knew there was nothing left at the scene of the crime, and now his life depended on how well he could play Urvi. She wasn't someone who would succumb to his charm, nor was she gullible like Molina. All he could do now was own up to his folly and make every promise in the book to convince Urvi that he would never ever walk that road again. He would stay true to Molina, to their love and his vow to her. But he was afraid that even that might not work.

He caught up with Urvi right as she was hailing a cab. He went and stood in front of her with folded hands, eyes brimming with tears and a voice feeble with fear. It was the figure of a guy on his deathbed with no hope of another breath, seeking mercy and pardon. In no mood for any more theatricals, Urvi pushed him aside and advised, "Don't even bother."

"Please, please, please, Urvi. Please give me a chance to fix this mess. Please, Urvi. I beg of you. Please punish me in any way you find fit. I admit to my crime, and I should be punished. You know Molina is my life. You know I love her to death."

He looked and sounded sincere and somewhere in her heart Urvi knew he was. She knew he loved Molina. She never doubted that about him. In fact, she never doubted him ever about his intentions towards Molina. However, love can have different meanings and approaches for different people. And this approach didn't fit anywhere in her definition of love. And she was adamant that she wasn't going to change her take on it.

"It's not my call to take. You should know this. You are not playing with my life and my happiness. Someone else will take a fall for who you are, and it should be her decision if she wants to. My responsibility is to let her know what I know. Unlike you, I have a full throbbing conscience and betraying my loved ones has no place in it. It's not something I can live with."

She yet again tried to move away.

"Can we please sit somewhere, and you let me mend this? Please. For old times' sake. Please," he pleaded and stood waiting.

For old times' sake was what saved him the day.

She turned to him and just said, "You get this one chance as a repayment once for saving my friend's life. This is the one and only time you are awarded a consideration."

They went and sat in the nearest café they could find, as neither was looking for any desirable place to make their meeting more pleasurable. It was out and out an arbitrary meeting, and the sooner it got over, the better for both. This time, Urvi waited for him to speak. She had said whatever she needed to. It was his mess to clean, and she sat there wondering how he or anybody could make amends for such a blinding blunder.

"I know whatever I say will sound hollow and fake, especially right after the way you saw my loathsome self, but please believe me that my love for Molina is not fake, not hollow. I know I was a total jerk back in there, and this one stupidity could cost me my whole life's happiness. And I will understand if you never would want to trust me. I wouldn't trust myself if I were you. But the truth is, I blundered, I slipped, and I have no excuse for it. There is nothing I can say in my defence that can justify any of it. All that I can offer is my sincerest apology and my repentance. I can offer my head on a platter for you to do as you please."

He sat there with his eyes down, burdened with guilt and shame, not being able to meet hers. "Because I don't know myself if I should be forgiven. I just know that I am willing to do anything to be forgiven." He begged and begged for some more time and with some more conviction. She sat there attacking him and rejecting him. And neither seemed to budge. Eventually, both were exhausted and silent.

Sam's heart was racing in anticipation of the verdict. Urvi felt she was sitting on the bench and was expected to pass judgment.

Urvi's shock and anger were turning into concern and confusion. Confusion, what if Sam's love for Molina was as sincere as he claimed, and this was a one-off blooper by this mindless young man? Then wouldn't she be taking away that love from Molina if she had to mention this episode to her? She was aware that Molina was crazily in love with Sam, and so far, it seemed that he was besotted with her. Theirs was a perfect world. Would she be wrong in shaking that world? On the other hand, her concern was, what if Sam turned out to be a serial offender? The unfaithful kind, the adulterous kind, the kind that you hear about, and the kind that never stops hurting the woman he claims to love because he is irreparably flawed.

Urvi went back and forth in her head with no success. Her young mind was too scared to go in either direction. One way was towards a confirmed immediate heartbreak, and another was a probable future one. After prolonged reasoning, she came to conclude that she would not ruffle the feathers then, and as for the future, she would make sure he didn't dare to make the same mistake ever again. She'd hold him hostage. She would make Sam sign a bond. If he wanted to stick around, he would have to. Else, he could very well go.

"If what you proclaim is really your truth, then convince me. Tell me, to what extent you can go to mortgage yourself? Prove it to me that you are ready to go to any length to make atonement. I need some insurance and some indemnity since your words are not enough, as you have just proved yourself. So, mere words are out. It has to be in writing. It has to be a sign and a sealed promise of love and loyalty. And since now the onus of safeguarding Molina's entire future is on me, you sure would understand that I am not leaving anything to chance." She tried to make her stand clear.

"I completely understand. And I also understand your need for some kind of assurance that you can throw at my face if I end up making any further mess. I get it. I seriously do. You tell me what's on your mind, and I will abide by it." With the little ray of hope in his direction, he finally gathered some courage to look up. Meeting her eyes, he said earnestly, "Whatever it takes, Urvi, whatever it takes."

Did he ever regret saying those words will never be known, but it's anybody's guess how in the future, they resulted in Urvi's only respite.

She mulled over the proposition long and hard, and her taking so much time may have made the already frightened Sam more alarmed, for when she said,

"A prenup. You gotta sign a prenup."

She took a chance and dropped the bomb. The only way she thought she could safely guard her credulous friend was by putting a golden gun to his head.

“Sure, anything.”

He jumped at the rope that he thought might save him from falling. “If a prenup can bring back your trust, then prenup it is.”

Losing Molina seemed worse than losing money, or so it seemed at that time. Most prenups are drawn with the confidence of happily ever after. And that’s what Sam always believed would be the case with Molina. Molina was too much into him to ever leave him. And he couldn’t dream of a life without her. They were meant to be together, and they would be together forever.

A prenup was agreed upon, and the episode was thus buried.

***

CHAPTER 13
AT THE CLINIC

Urvi got up and pulled Molina from her trance. They needed to get out of the place and never return. The place was suffocating her. She felt it was closing down on her and soon was going to crush them both. She was standing up but couldn't feel her legs. She tried to put them forward, but they refused. Just then, she found herself being pulled back on the chair. Molina sat there with a hint of a smile on her face, which didn't reach her eyes. But it definitely was a smile. She had a defiant and assertive smile, and she said, "We will finish what we came here for."

Urvi didn't try to get up again. Now that Molina spoke, they'd better have a talk. And then, there was a smile. A smile was not good. Not on her, and certainly not right now. How could there be a smile?

"We will finish, but some other time, not today. I need to get out of here. We need to get out. We are upset, hurt, and angry, and we have a right to be. You should be out somewhere screaming and crying, abusing and cursing. You should be breaking things around you. You should be going after that bastard and beating the shit out of him!" Urvi stopped to take a breath in. The accumulated fury erupted ferociously and made her feel lighter. Molina needed to let it out, too.

"Let's sit somewhere for a light meal, or if you want privacy, we can go to my place. But we are definitely getting out of here."

Her tone was firm and decisive. Under other circumstances Molina would have followed her out without a protest. She was not one for arguments or disagreements. She was easy and flexible, even to a fault. And it was not for the lack of opinion or want. She just was okay with mostly anything as she managed to find something to love and enjoy in everything.

But being okay with what had just happened was not okay. Urvi, who knew Molina well enough to understand her take on all things suddenly had a surprise coming.

"I have been vigilant, and I know we are next. We can't let our wait go to waste. Besides, you have stolen my morning me-time, so it better be of some use." Already half-dazed, both had no energy left to argue. They sat and waited.

Urvi went through the ordeal with the doctor half-heartedly. She gave a sample for them to test again and she heard them say it was positive. She found Molina hugging her and whispering something in a cheerful tone. There was a genuine gleam in Molina' eyes and the smile lighted her face. Of course, Urvi was going to have a baby and Molina couldn't be 'not thrilled'. From the look of it, all seemed well in their world.

Once they stepped outside, Urvi didn't know which way to go. What course to take. If Molina had been reflecting any signs of anguish or heartbreak that is expected in a situation like this, Urvi would have known how to deal with it. But this protective layer of denial and the heroic cover of courage was making her scared. It felt like she was walking on landmines, and it was impossible to look for triggers.

"Where to?" She left it to Molina to take the next step forward.

"You need to spoil me, you know?" said Molina.

Of course, I need to, but not for the reason you are suggesting, Urvi thought.

But instead said, "Whatever for?"

If Molina didn't want any pity or sympathy, she would not give her any. She also would play along if that's what helped Molina. "I should be the one getting spoilt."

"Not a chance. It's all thanks to my prayers that we got to see this day."

As she uttered these words, the irony of it struck her and Urvi. Clearly God wasn't listening to her prayers or else she wouldn't have seen this day. Not like this. Not in its totality. This wasn't the day she prayed for. Who would pray for a day like this?

Quickly recovering, she suggested, "The weather is lovely. Let's go to the rooftop of Sobo House."

"You are the boss." Not wanting to complicate matters further, Urvi concluded.

***

CHAPTER 14
STARING AT REALITY

Certain fears are very sporadic and have a tendency to disappear, leaving no trace of occupying any place in your life, but they can return with full velocity as if they had never left. Urvi's fears also bid adieu soon after Molina and Sam settled into matrimony. Molina flaunted the happy glow on her face as she returned from her honeymoon and was exceptionally chatty and buoyant. She carried an air of sureness and certitude, which came from being in a good place. It also spoke of Sam in a good light without any words spoken.

With respect to Urvi, her binoculars were out and zooming. The apprehension mixed with guilt kept her antennas up, and she closely watched Molina and Sam together for the first few months of their marriage. What she didn't know was that Sam was watching her too, watching him. And though it was not an act that he put up to be Molina's please machine, he did notice Urvi's intrusive gaze sizing him up and down, time and again. It made him uncomfortable and, worse still, guarded. His constant efforts to be a loving and indulgent husband, ceaselessly proving his devotion and loyalty, did sow the seeds for his upcoming proficiency in pretence and deception. His heart was in the right place as far as Molina was concerned, but his excessive gesticulations and verbal outpour of love were extended to Urvi and Urvi alone. So, it was Urvi who drew out the willingness in him, and the outcome gave him the confidence to further his reach.

***

A chilling nervousness was taking over her. Their friendship had been one of fun and mirth. They had only bliss and harmony between them. But this was different. That day was different. The space between them was filled with fear for the struggle that lay ahead, to gather the nerve to collect the broken pieces and make them whole. They were not used to it.

She held Molina's hand and proceeded towards the car park. She was half expecting Sam lurking around somewhere in the shadows behind one of the cars. She was sure he must have wanted to see the debris caused by his cruel, cowardly act. She didn't want to take chances. "I will drive now."

She put out her hand for the keys. She would take her to Sobo, Molina's favourite hangout. The place always lifted her mood. They settled near the window that was overlooking the beach. Even better. Without wasting any time, Urvi picked up the conversation. There was no point dilly-dallying any more. She had to get to the point and get it over and done with. She reached out across the table and took Molina's hands into hers. "Now what?" she wondered aloud.

No prelude was needed. No drama, no outbursts, no complaining, no cursing could help it. Neither any philosophizing, rationalizing or normalizing could justify it. Why waste time and energy on the bygones? Begin from that moment itself and do the best that you can for yourself. She had learned this from Molina. Give your all to the solution, and the problem will crumple under its weight on its own.

"Hmmm… just a salad for me, please," she said calmly. If anyone saw Molina, there was no telling that her world had just collapsed. That she just got stabbed in the back and that her heart was writhing in excruciating pain. She was sitting like she was sitting in meditation, with a serene look on her face, surrounded by unimaginable peace.

"You will get your salad." She signalled to the waiter and ordered one salad each and their preferred coffees. "Now, let's talk about what just happened back there."

She looked straight into Molina's eyes, giving her no leeway to sidestep. "I will not let you pretend you are the same person that you woke up as in the morning. That you will go home, like always, and live happily ever after."

Urvi spoke with the firmness that Molina had never experienced. She sat there unable to react and respond. Seeing her passively sitting with no trace of an emotion, Urvi's frustration started mounting.

"Can you at least say something? Can you please open your mouth and let your feelings out? You have to. There is no one coming to collect the rubble that has been thrown at you and clean up your heart and headspace for you. It's no one but you and I. And unless you open up, even I can't do shit."

She was getting more and more alarmed by the extended silence and stillness and was worried this might turn into a case of selective traumatic mutism. She had seen, in movies and even read in books, how mutism led to worsened anxiety. It could cause an irreparable inability to live an emotionally normal life, and the result was difficulties in developing personal relationships.

She would have to make Molina talk. Let her release the lava that was accumulating on her gutted insides. She may not yet have realized its devastating reach, but Urvi knew it would seep in slowly into every pore of her psyche and gradually damage and scar her for life.

Molina was looking out at the ocean through the window of the café. The waves were so calm as though the sea was in siesta. Its smoothness was conveying the state of Molina's mind. It appeared to be so calm and comforting yet it was so vast and deep. It hid so much beneath it yet looked like a widespread flat sheet. Urvi was not sure if the stillness and quiet was healing or it was suppressing. She made another attempt.

"Molina, I am getting worried here. You better start talking. Like right now. I need you to barf out your ire, wrath, and your outrage. Let's talk about the bastard. Talk about us wanting to kill him. Talk about the most horrendous torture we could subject him to. You know he is not going scot-free. He will have to pay, and he will have to pay big."

She tried to say all that she was expecting Molina to say so as to open the floodgates of her bottled-up anguish and misery. The pain had to find a way out of her system. If it stayed in, Molina would never be the same again. "The first step is that you are packing his bags and throwing him out of the house."

"No, I am not. He is not going anywhere," she said as if she was giving a verdict. "As for the rest, I will take my time to decide."

And the verdict concluded.

"What? Are you going to let that bastard walk back into your life? As if he had just gone for a walk in the park and, on the way back, picked up a woman and a baby, like they were a bag of groceries and handed them over to you, and you will make a place for them in your life?"

"He has not gone anywhere to walk back in. He has always been here, at home. Living in that house. Been there for eight years."

"So, he continues living like nothing happened? You continue living with him like all is okay?" Urvi shrugged her shoulders and shook her head like she couldn't believe what she was hearing. "Perfect!" she sighed.

"I know I am going to do right by myself, and you will learn it in time to come."

"What do you mean? What's going on in your mind? What are you planning?"

Since Urvi couldn't wrap her head around anything solvable at this moment, this 'In time to come' sounded a bit leery and she eyed Molina with suspicion.

"You will see," and Molina left it at that.

And she knew that was all she would get, at least for the moment.

***

CHAPTER 15
THE AFFAIR

Ridden with guilt, shame, fear and helplessness, Sam drove back as silent and stiff as a stone. There was no conversation to be made. There was nothing that could be said by any of the two riding in the car, as they both knew the predicament was self-inflicted. They both were two mature adults who knowingly fell prey to their callousness. They shamelessly fed their greed, their lust, and their ego with complete disregard for the repercussions. They knew that the fire that they were igniting to warm themselves up would eventually charge innocent lives, including theirs. Yet they went ahead, and here they were, sitting on top of the wreckage and wondering how to clean up.

Sam's head was hanging limp like a balloon that ran out of its air. The woman in question, Sabrina, was looking ahead onto the road as if trying to see where her life was going. The tension between them was sharp enough to cut through a rock and silence was the only shield that could save them at that moment in time.

Crippled with horror and remorse, Sam pulled over the car outside Sabrina's apartment building and sat there as if life had been sucked out of him. Sabrina knew better than to say anything and quietly got out and waited by the window for any sign of life. But there was none.

She wondered whether she should ask him to come in. She saw no point. She still lived with her parents, and there was no way she could have offered him even a day's shelter. Theirs started as a clandestine affair, and he was not allowed inside her house ever. And in the present scenario, he wouldn't have been welcome even if he did. Sabrina's family followed certain principles, but a married man in their daughter's life absolutely wasn't one of them. Sabrina's defiance to go ahead with the pregnancy against their wishes had not gone down well with them. They took it as a jolt to their values and maintained a no-support stance all through.

For Sam, he was being penalized for his debaucheries and with a noose of blackmail around his neck in this regard. His decisions were not his anymore.

His logical reasoning and tireless pleadings fell on Sabrina's deaf ears, as she was hell-bent on keeping the baby. She had tasted the good life and had been enjoying the luxuries of being the girlfriend of a successful man. The kid was her ticket to the continuation of that, and she knew she wasn't going back to her lower-middle-class life ever. Friends and family be damned.

With no support from her family and anyone else for that matter, she sat comfortably on Sam's shoulder. He tried every possible way to bail himself out of the tangle. He had got into it just to have some fun; she, too, seemed like she was out to live it up. Like most stupid men, Sam thought that he would be smart and that he would wade through this deceitful life without a hitch. He would have his fun on the side, be a dutiful, devoted husband to his lovely wife and an indulgent, caring dad to his child. This is how it plays out in a man's world. Some are seasoned regulars, and they seem to manage just fine. Others brave it out once in a while, but they do.

But what nobody tells you is how it ends. Where does it end, whenever it ends? There is no mention of the slide down. The crash landing and the eventual downfall. You just get to see the shine. You don't get to see the tattered lives that lie in its wake.

He learnt it the hard way and it was his cross to bear. Only that day he felt the loosening up of the noose. But the cross got heavier.

After waiting for a minute or so and seeing no movement from Sam, she realized that her days of power were over. She no longer had the ace up her sleeve, and now Sam was free to do as he pleased. And she knew in her heart, what it was going to be. She turned and walked back into her building. Let it sort itself out was all she told herself.

***

Their dalliance had started on a typical shoddy note. It couldn't be called a love affair, as both were drunk, reckless, crass and full of lust. A young, successful man with new money flowing out of his pockets often seeks approval for his stature by drawing the attention of any young, attractive woman, who herself was measuring the seductive power of her beauty by enticing any wealthy man. Two predators. Two most predictable candidates. Two habitual offenders. It's astonishing how smoothly and effortlessly two people agree to jump into the well of passion, knowing the climb out of it will scratch them, bleed them and may even cripple them.

Sam and Sabrina had eyed each other for most of the evening at Yash's promotion bashes, who was his employee. It wasn't a big celebration, and Molina wasn't really required to be there. So, she sat this one out like she did most times when she knew she wouldn't be missed. Sam was never the insistent kind, which helped. Sabrina came in as the younger sister to Yash's wife's business partner. They were into flowers, and they had done a little bit of jazzing up the place. Sabrina was helping her sister out as the other partner spent the day trying to look her best. It was her husband's day, after all. As a courtesy, Sabrina was asked to join them, and after finishing the job, the sisters went back home to get ready. Sabrina had heard a lot about Sam's sudden rise up the success ladder, and she took a good amount of time to dress. All this delayed them by a good hour or so, and they made a late entry to the party.

There is something about late entries. Especially if you are a looker and if it's a buzzing party. People already there are bored and exhausted looking at the same faces, and every time a new one enters, most eyes dart towards it, filled with anticipation of something exciting and new. Most are expecting some glamour and glitz. When Sabrina entered with her sister, she brought both and in abundance. Soon, all eyes were on her. Men, for what she brought with her, and women, for why she was even there.

Sam didn't take long to notice her effect in the room and picked up the eye contact game before anyone else could. Sabrina, on her part, took her time. She had yet to survey the crowd and make her choice. But she did take a mental note of him. Her snub or indifference made Sam determined to score. He was the boss of this place and his imaginary kingdom. And she had wandered into his realm. He tried the teasing game by flirting with other women and somehow made sure that she was in earshot. Partly that worked, and partly the fact that he happened to be the one who ticked most boxes for a night of fun. And so, it began. It was a plain, simple night of fun by two very willing individuals who didn't plan to take it anywhere beyond the night. A one-night stand, and you go your separate ways. At least, that's what Sam told himself. And what Sabrina must have expected.

Unfortunately for Sam, he ended up leaving a more lasting impression on Sabrina than he would have wanted, and she didn't hesitate to admit to being the one wanting more of him. To make it even worse, she turned out to be a chaser. The ambitious girl who never dithered to go after what she desired, and Sam was whom she desired. Initially, the attention from a pretty young girl did him well, and he went along with flirting and texting. He was the man who liked to have his occasional fun but was shrewd enough to cut the cord just when he realized it was time to call it a day. But years of experience made him complacent, and he became confident that he would walk away at his will. He had been doing that, and he would go on doing that. Her insistence on meeting sounded more like a challenge, and initially, Sam took it up as just that. One coffee date, and they took it from where they had left. She would dare him, and he would get sucked into it. Soon, it became a game of thrill and adventure; days seemed intriguing, and life became exciting.

Sabrina had no rear-view mirror to look back into, so she kept her sight fixed ahead on the joy ride with Sam. She was living her dream at the young age of twenty-one; she was enjoying the life of a well-heeled man's woman, or so she believed. Her demand for time and attention grew, and along with it grew expectations and confrontations. In a few months' time, Sam had begun to feel stifled. He knew where it was going, and he had no mind going that way. He was preparing the groundwork for a smooth, clean breakup, which would look like her idea to her, and she'd cut him loose on her own. He knew which card to play and was already feeling like a winner when Sabrina broke the news of her pregnancy. His sins finally bore fruition and would be on display in no time.

He was standing at the edge of a cliff, and the only way out was down.

***

CHAPTER 16
THE FALLOUT

There should be a guidebook on infidelity. For unfaithful men, for adulterous kind, who knew their way in but couldn't figure their way out. The kind who lost a home without securing another, the kind who bargained lifelong happiness for short-term fun and who went to grab it all. And lost it all.

Sam drove around aimlessly and thoughtlessly till he couldn't anymore. He had to stop somewhere sometime. He parked the car a few yards away from his house and sat staring at the once-happy home of his. The structure looked the same, giving away very little of the devastation inside. He tried to gauge the mood.

But Sam, a wicked, merciless, depraved man outside these walls?

His entire life flashed before him. He used to be a young, promising guy, and he lived up to that promise. He achieved exactly what was expected of him, or maybe more. In his parents' eyes, he had made them proud. He didn't remember ever disobeying them or anyone else. He thought he was doing everything right by the book, and he had been made to feel that way, too. He was cultured, warm, generous, considerate, compassionate and charitable. He was admired and loved. He brought happiness and cheer to people. That was who he was.

Then who was this Sam? Who was this Sam, who was none of the above? Who was this disappointment, this failure, and this disaster? Who?

This was not the Sam she loved. This was not the Sam she deserved. This Sam was not worthy of her. She deserved better. She was promised better. Unable to face her, he took his second stupid decision of the day. He shamefully deserted the scene and drove away to find a roof over his head to spend the night in repentance.

As if whatever happened wasn't enough, Sam not returning home at all made it even worse. In such situations, the culprit sincerely seeking forgiveness and mercy may have a hope for salvation and a chance if the appeal is made sooner than later. The victim gets little or no chance to replay and rethink. There is no time to weigh the pros and cons. There is no time to get used to the absence and its eventual realization that the absence works just fine. Also, the eagerness and persistence to make amends often softens the target. And the pardon is likely to land in your lap easily.

Yet there is a flip side to it, too. Often, decisions taken and pardons given in haste later result in dissatisfaction and displeasure. And having the luxury of time to go back and forth, there is a scope to alter your ruling.

In this case may be the former approach would have been more apt, though there is no saying what would have worked; if at all.

Sam not returning was taken as a sign that he had jumped the fence to the other side. That he chose to stick by his misdeeds. Forget about shame, guilt and repentance; his lack of care and concern for her well-being after this devastating betrayal dug the wound deeper. She wanted to imagine him at her feet, face drowning in tears and heart bleeding with the pain that he caused her. When you hurt someone you love, you hurt more. That is the beauty of love. That should have been the beauty of their love.

Sitting by her favourite kitchen window, Molina ran her mind through the events of the day. A quick recap and a quick conclusion vis a vis her life. Urvi had threatened to be back in a jiffy. She had gone to pack the weeklong bag of her essentials, but Molina was not given a choice. She wasn't sure if right now she would have been better off alone or if she could actually use a shoulder. But she understood Urvi. Molina wouldn't have left Urvi alone had the scene been reversed. She had, in fact, taken Urvi out on a weekend after her one major breakup. She was going to be in good hands, she told herself.

With her heart still pounding in anticipation of the ugliness that would follow the existing ugliness, she let her thoughts take her to all possible ways the coming days could unfold. What happened was not what needed to be pondered over. She could go on telling herself over and over again that she got cheated and deceived by her loving husband. That, this loving husband of hers, loved someone else now. That the husband was going to be having a child with another woman, and that her stable home was shaken from its roots and her marriage was now broken. She could go on and on, and it wouldn't change. There was no hand that could seal the crack and no magic wand that could undo the pain. What was done was done. Now, what needed to be done had to be her call. She was not going to wait, watch and improvise. Her time was starting at that moment. It was right then that she would have to resolve what course to adopt to get herself justice and what she had to do to heal herself.

She was not the confrontational type. She was not given to outbursts and showdowns. Fighting and grabbing was not her way to acquire something. She believed in doing whatever was the right thing to do and the outcome was hers to accept or reject. That power she kept in her hand.

She knew she would not yell, question, blame or abuse. She herself wouldn't be able to handle the melodrama. Nor would she give her marriage another chance. She would not open her arms to a repenting husband, nor would she let him make it up to her. She would do none of that, yet as and when Sam walked in, if he walked in, the doors would be open for him.

And as she sat thinking, a big smile originated at the corner of her lips, spread across her face and rested there. She had settled on how she was going to seek her revenge.

***

CHAPTER 17
PICKING UP THE PIECES

Urvi's anxiety was hitting the roof. What was going on with Molina? Why was she so normal? Why was she grinning so much? As soon as Urvi arrived, she went straight up to the guest room to unpack and arrange her belongings. When she walked in, she could swear that the room had been sprayed with Molina's favourite freshener minutes back. She saw a vase with fresh flowers on the bedside table, fresh towels, and a water jug by the bedside. The space didn't look like it belonged to a heartbroken, distraught soul that needed comforting and consoling.

Perplexed, she came down and saw what she had felt. Molina was playing soft music on her phone. The table was set for dinner with finery. More nicely done than Urvi remembered from her previous umpteen casual dinners. She checked the setting to see any sign of disorientation or neglect, but there were none. All the sauces, pickles, and condiments were neatly arranged and wow... there were candles, too. Molina was warming the food, and a bottle of champagne was waiting in the bucket to be opened.

Urvi literally stopped in her tracks. Was Molina losing it? Wasn't she dealing with her trauma a wee bit oddly? Urvi had seen in the movies how shock-ridden people resort to denial as a shield to protect themselves from the heart-wrenching ache that threatens to devour them. And in the bargain, they hit the extreme high that borderlines to insanity. She could take care of a broken-hearted, hurting, wailing Molina, as that would have been the predictable response needing a predictable approach. With an arm around for support, a heart to care and a promise to ride through the tide together, she was sure they would have found their footing.

***

Urvi took the champagne glass in her hands and quizzed, "So, clearly, we are in a celebratory mood with a bottle of bubbly and all. And what are we celebrating here again?"

She tried to be sarcastic, even a bit nasty, in the hope that it might stir up some required and desired effect. "Your husband's new baby? His secret lover or your sorry state?"

"It's champagne. Champagne that you pop to celebrate happy milestones in your life." She ignored the instigation and kept her disposition composed. She poured the champagne into two glasses. One much less than the other, and Urvi looked at her perplexed. Molina handed her the one with less champagne, picked up hers and went, "Cheers to the one soon mom-to-be and one godmother-to-be. This is what we are celebrating, in case you forgot. And excuse me if this isn't a reason enough for you, but for me, nothing can dampen my spirit, not even the end of my marriage. So, you and me, baby, we have to raise our glasses and begin welcoming a little angel into our hearts."

The sincerity and genuineness in her demeanour and her voice made Urvi's heart ache even more.

"I hope you know you are only getting to drink this much and no more," Molina chided and filled her own glass. "I will drink for the two of us and do a lot, many more things too, for the two of us. You just chill, enjoy and give us a healthy baby."

"I can see that, my darling, and I can also see what my next eight months will look like. Be my guest. Go ahead and finish the bottle. We better have a story to tell your godchild," Urvi said grumpily, but in her heart, she was secretly relieved that Molina was unwinding and loosening.

"We should. We should have a story to tell, and we should also have to make lovely memories to cherish."

Her reasoning was the balm that she was applying to her sinking heart, and as long as it made enough sense to her to help keep her floating toward the shore, it was good enough.

Molina's philosophical take only confused Urvi more, as she couldn't connect its relevance to the day's episode. She had come with a bag and baggage to comfort and console Molina, but here she was, sitting and being tutored on taking life by its collar. In all fairness, Urvi thought she would fall into the first category of people who were in the middle of the party. If it weren't for the day's disastrous discovery, the day would have been all about her. After years of waiting, her dream was being fulfilled. But she kept her joy aside to help Molina collect the pieces of her shattered dreams.

"Rightly said. So here it is. I am waiting for a tiny winy refill if you please."

She waved her glass in front of Molina, and she obliged with a tiny winy fill.

"Cheers!" Urvi said, finally picking up the matter for which she was supposed to be here. "Okay, either we stay up all night and explore this freshly acquired wisdom of yours, or we start being wise by addressing the elephant in the room? Your choice entirely. But just remember, stalling is not going to make it disappear, and you may think you would be able to carry the load all on your lean shoulders and reach the other side undamaged. But trust me, I am what you will need every step of the way. So please, let's not hide behind the curtain. You got to be out with it."

The stern look and the grave tone of her voice told Molina the party was over, and it was time for business. She would have to face the reality sooner or later. She would have to take a stable, undeviating and unwavering call on what would be the best course of action for her personal well-being and, at the same time, befitting to her son's complete welfare. There was not going to be any suffering of any kind in her son's life that could be traced back to this episode, and his world would stay as pristine and perfect as she always wanted it to be. She wouldn't suffer, and her son wouldn't either.

She would think of something. She knew she was capable of saving herself and her son, and she knew she would not fail them both.

"I will reduce the size of the elephant to a tiny ant, and soon, you won't even notice its presence. Let me have some time to process this jolt. All I can promise you is that you will be neither disappointed nor ashamed once I have chosen my battle."

***

CHAPTER 18
BACK HOME, YET NOT

It took almost a week for Sam to gather the courage to appear at the front door of their house. One early morning, he rang the doorbell and turned to walk back to the other side of the road. He preferred to observe the welcome from afar. He wasn't scared of any violence or showdown. He was just scared to see the hurt and pain on Molina's face. His past week had gone in him kicking himself every single moment and finding ways for reparation. And there was nothing that he thought would be able to salvage this situation. He thought it best to put himself at Molina's mercy. And there he was, standing facing the door to his once-happiest place on earth.

He heard the sound of the opening of the door, but his eyes refused to cooperate. They were too terrified to look up and were staring at his feet, which were glued to the ground. Moments passed, and no sound could be heard that was directed at him, nor one of the doors closing. He picked up the nerve to look up, and there she was, standing like a shadow inside the wide-open door. She stood there, revealing nothing. A moment passed, and as their eyes met, she turned and walked back in.

Leaving the door… still… wide open.

If a door is shut in your face and says you're not wanted, then isn't a door left wide open to say you could come in?

Sam saw her walking in as if leaving a trail of invitation. In any other scenario, this would have been a very seductive and provocative offer but Sam knew today it meant anything but. It looked like a death trap and he felt enormously perplexed to where it would lead. He wished he could rewind and redo his past ten months. He wished.

Knowing it was now or never, he took one step at a time, like treading on water. He wanted to go nowhere but inside, yet never wanted to reach the door. But he did, and according to him, it was too fast. He stepped inside and immediately felt like a stranger. His familiar home of eight years strangely bore the look of a spa, and the comforting solace of the place had Zen-like vibes with fresh flowers, scented candles and soothing devotional music playing in the dimly lit lounge. He had come in prepared to enter a dishevelled, gloomy place. This unaffected and enhanced space threw him totally off-balance. He spotted Molina by the electric kettle and saw she was making tea. He went into the kitchen and waited by the door. She filled up a cup and then another, and he realized that there was no one else in the room besides them both. The other cup was, but of course, meant for him, and he felt a little life returning to him. She walked up to where he was standing, kept the teacup by the countertop near him, and left the room.

What was that? What did it mean?

She let him in; she served him tea and left him hanging there. With no sign of what his fate was going to be, he was left to interpret all of it on his own. He picked up the cup and walked to the back of the house and sat down on the stone bench in the garden.

With no movement, no dialogue, and no visual action towards him, he lingered around the back for a while before he thought it best to resume his presence in the house the way it had been. He decided to wait for Molina to break the silence. He had no heart to make any move. He couldn't take a chance with another false note.

She was sitting on her laptop and writing some mails or so he gathered. He quietly went into their bedroom and quickly stepped into the shower. The bathroom finally felt familiar. The scent of his favourite soap, the accustomed feel of his towel and the rhythm of the water, falling over his body. He was home. The conflicting emotions of relief and dread were similar to the combination of the hot water mixed with a cold that was pouring over him.

Breakfast was laid on the dining table for him like it had been all their married years, but the dining table was not as crowded as it had always been. A single plate was served, lonesome, unaccompanied, undecorated. It depicted his present state and future status at his home. The empty vastness of the remaining table comprised what lay ahead of him. He stood looking at it and fought the unsettling emotions of this unwelcoming welcome. He went to the study and found her eating a bowl of cereal, still working in front of the laptop. He had made his entry loud to make his presence not go unnoticed. But her eyes stayed fixed on the screen, and her body defiantly unflinching. It was clear she was avoiding him, and he thought it was for the better. He had no answer to give her, no excuse to offer and no reasoning to justify. If it took time and got buried this way, he couldn't be happier.

He silently celebrated her silence.

He told himself he could live with it.

If only he knew how this silence would deafen him for the rest of his life.

Molina went about the house like she had been all these years, and nothing but nothing sent a message that anything was amiss except for her silence. She didn't utter a word, and Sam couldn't dare. Her mute stand was communicating her refusal to entertain any subject related or not related to Sam's misdeeds. His first day after his return went by in anticipation of an upcoming dialogue, but nothing came about. Unsure of his position in the house and in her life, he waited to be told his every step forward. But the visuals left no clues about following the lead. From finding his breakfast, lunch, tea and dinner, all laid out at the appointed time with precision, to spotting his side of the bedside table with a fresh jug of water, his pillows intact in their place on their bed, it all appeared like a smooth welcome back. Only he knew it was anything but. After spending the entire day staring at the vacuum, he finally braved inside their bedroom. There, Molina was sleeping as usual on her side of the bed, with what looked like enough place left to occupy for him to sleep. His heart was pounding vigorously and was threatening to skip out of him, and his mind was a ball of mess. It was beyond impossible to contemplate the outcome of the decision that needed to be taken. Was it going to be that night or never? Was this the moment of crucifixion? Should he proceed to walk on fire and get it over and done with?

He decided to put his head in the lion's mouth and slipped into the room and into bed.

He lay there, barely breathing, fearing he would wake her up. He had to pass through just that night. The morning would affirm the verdict on his boundaries.

***

CHAPTER 19
REFLECTION

He was fortunate to have overslept. Maybe it was the fear of not wanting to face the next day or the exhaustion of living in panic all these days, but he was out till almost noon, and when he came down the stairs, he found the house empty. Molina had left for work. The maid must have cleaned and cleared the workload. He looked for any note, any instruction, but there was none. He contemplated and thought it best to make a small workstation in a corner of the guest room. In his mind, his constant presence in the house would help assure Molina that the other chapter of his life was over. That he was hers and hers alone, and his life was she and their son. He was not going anywhere and to no one. His disgusting, wild days were a thing of the past, and he had realized the worth of a family by nearly losing it.

He had neither met nor spoken to Sabrina nor had she called him. With changed dynamics now, both were on different footings than before and he knew he was the decision maker in all of this for a change. And he had decided to not sacrifice his home for what he thought was a big mistake. He would provide financial support, but if anyone has to be a single parent to a child, it had to be Sabrina and not Molina.

He was not used to fending for himself at home but he was ready to learn. He was ready to do everything in his power to bring back the house to its original bliss. He had killed it. He would bring it back to life.

***

The following couple of weeks passed in the exact manner as his first day. Things went on like they always used to, except for communication, which was still non-existent. The slight improvement was that there were written exchanges of notes to inform one another of whatever needed to be done. The silent treatment was killing Sam, and though he did try to make several attempts to converse by greeting a good morning, a good night, or a see you, it didn't bear any fruit. Urvi had blocked him on her phone and pretty much in her life, too. She came by the house almost every day; in fact, she spent most of her time at their place whenever Molina was home, yet he was invisible to her. His only solace was the company of his son, and gradually, all his free time got diverted to the kid. He got more involved in his life, and the house became a little bearable to live in.

Sabrina's baby arrived during this phase of intense conflict, and Sam found himself at the crossroads yet again.

The archetypal dilemma of an adulterer.

The age-old predicament is one in which there is no right way out.

***

The question in such scenarios is, how many casualties can one avoid? The only choice left to make is, who can be comparatively saved, and whose pain can be reduced? There is no whitewash that can hide the stains. No thread that can stitch the wound and no glue that can join the cracks.

What a terrible place to be in.

What a crushing decision to make.

The only thing that made it possible for Sam to pick a side was the fact that he was in no way guilty of encouraging or misleading Sabrina. In fact, it was the other way around. He was verbally and intentionally very clear from day one that their hook-up was a result of two adults giving in to an impulsive, spur-of-the-moment sexual attraction towards each other, and nothing should be expected out of it. He had made it abundantly known that he was not only happily married but that he loved his wife dearly and that his escapade was no indication that he was out for a long run in the field. What followed was a chase solely on the part of Sabrina, and each time he gave in, he hinted that that was the end of it and that there would be no more. His stand was firm every single time. He called themselves both 'strangers with benefits'. One day, the benefits turned into major losses, and he became a stranger to his own wife.

Also, the fact that he was not in favour of her keeping the child and had categorically told Sabrina that he would not be a party to it gave him a clean chit in his mind. He got embroiled in extending his presence and support during the proceeding months purely on the basis of the threat of disclosure to his wife. The entire episode was nothing less than tormenting for him, and now, with the peril losing its steam, he was ready to close the door on Sabrina.

If he had to give any legal compensation, he was ready for it. But he would provide nothing personal or emotional.

He had made up his mind.

From now on, it was only going to be all about Molina and his son.

If there was a decision that came a wee bit late in the day, it was this.

***

CHAPTER 20
FOR THE SON

The normalcy in the house had to do with their son Veer. Anything to do with his routine, his requirements and his demands. The one thing that had been stopping Sam from putting everything out on the table for Molina to release her withheld feelings was just the fear of making it worse for their son. He knew that she knew. She knew that he knew she knew. She didn't bring it up at all and continued to not only stay under the same roof and sleep in the same bed, but she also never lost her cool on him, never taunted him or made life difficult for him.

Veer was the fortunate offspring of abundantly gifted parents and grandparents. And he was further fortunate to inherit the best from them all. Physical or otherwise, he picked the most desirable attributes there were to pick from and added some more attractive traits. Both sides treated Veer differently and sometimes even preferentially, and she became careful that Veer never caught any hint of that. It never did well for a child to get favours that other kids didn't enjoy. Veer had his mother's soft curls and lithe frame, yet Sam's athletic frame gave him a good mix of charm and strength. He was encouraged and commended yet advised and corrected. It kept a good balance, and he was growing up with his head firmly on his shoulders.

His happy world was intact underneath the earthquake that shattered his parent's world.

In all of this, Veer's birthday arrived. Like every year, that year too, the planning took place with full enthusiasm and devotion, but mostly through correspondence and signs and gestures. Urvi was hands-on, and it became easier for Sam as he left the money for the bills that he found lying on the table or were texted to him. Veer had been so well attended, entertained and indulged at home that he had no inkling about the woes of the house. Both his parents were a call away, were chirpier than ever and had never been so eager to please him. Molina wanted him to be unaffected at any cost, and she succeeded by avoiding any drama. Sam, too, realized that the peace in the house was thanks to the kid, and he was completely attuned to it.

The day of his birthday was the first time after the debacle that Molina and Sam were to face the outside world together. Sam's apprehensions about the eyes on them made him immensely nervous, and he called up Urvi's husband, Jay, to join them for support. He had no clue how much he knew about their state of affairs, as Sam had been keeping an absolutely low profile. But he now thought he needed to know and learn to face it. And what better way to start than on his own home ground?

The evening began with the usual fanfare that a kid's birthday requires. Kids on one side exploring and enjoying the fun and games, mothers standing by their side watching keenly. Men disinterested and bored were giving occasional approving and encouraging glances towards their offspring. The typical, predictable, identical, pattern of human existence was on full display.

It was after the party was over and when just a few of the adults had stayed back that Jay noticed the tension between his wife and Sam and soon after between Molina and Sam. Unsure of his readings, he gave himself some more time to observe if his instincts were indeed right. He was aware that his wife and Sam had been thick since their teenage years, and they had their own equation away from Molina. When no exchange of words took place between these two for the rest of the evening, he felt it was time he got into the middle of it. He stood next to Urvi and expressed his concerns.

"What's going on, Urvi? I can see that you are avoiding Sam and that things don't seem to be all okay with Molina and Sam, too. What could be so terrible that you guys are not talking to Sam at all? You three are the ultimate unbreakable trio, and I am a little worried about you guys here."

"If you are worried about Sam, don't be. He has too many people in his life to worry about him. As for Mols and me, we are enough for each other."

She tried to cut short the conversation and started walking away, as she didn't want to divulge anything more without Molina's consent.

"Don't behave so childishly, Urvi. You don't break friendships and relations on a whim. This is too precious a bond to be allowed to disband. Love like what you all have happened to only very fortunate people."

He was earnestly trying to seek a truce.

"Then we are not very fortunate ones after all."

She laughed cynically and gestured for him to follow her towards the rest of the guests.

She knew that it couldn't be hidden from him anymore now that he had picked up on the case.

It became difficult for Jay to be comfortable around Sam, knowing he might be guilty of something awful and not knowing what it was. Jay was a fair guy on all accounts, and he preferred to have a balanced perspective on the occurrences in his life or even those personally unrelated to him. Hence, he spent the rest of the evening being cordial to Sam yet refrained from his usual overfriendly self. His eyes were on Molina more than on his wife. And as the evening came to a close, he read most of what ensued this change of equation on Molina's face. Sam sensed his awkwardness but didn't broach the topic, considering the unsuitable setting. He noticed Jay's extra warm and prolonged hug to Molina, and he knew the cat was soon going to be out of the bag.

The night ended with all four of them heavily ridden with a differently disturbing emotion.

Their happy days together were over.

***

CHAPTER 21
THE DISCLOSURE

Jay stayed up all night, distressed over what Urvi unveiled. First, he couldn't believe it. He and Sam had been great friends ever since he met him through Urvi. They hung out together as dating couples and later as married ones. And the easygoing Jay and Sam, the charmer, hit it off from day one. With both the girls literally joined at the hip personally and professionally, they saw a lot of each other and gradually formed their own rapport. Jay, being Jay, never detected any indication that Sam could ever be a dodgy guy on any front. The revelation came as a complete shocker to him. Sam? The guy he believed he knew inside out? The guy he could have bet on? The guy whom he secretly admired? It was his first disillusionment, and it kept him up.

There was no question in his mind whose side he was on. Not because of where he found his wife standing, but because he was a man of principles and for him the rule was simple; do no wrong, support no wrong.

Urvi found him with his cup of tea and an almost burnt toast lying by the side table of the relaxing chair he was swinging on. Deep in thought, he didn't hear her come. She went back into the kitchen and made herself a cup of tea and a few toasts, too. The conversation was going to be long, and she needed her cup of tea to last that long. She took the chair next to him and extended the plate of fresh toasts to him; he picked one and looked up at her with deep, pensive eyes. Urvi could see they were full of self-blame and hurt.

Urvi reached out and took his hands into hers and softly whispered, "You are not going to sit here and blame yourself. You were not holding his little finger and leading him through life. His life and his choices are his call, and he is the only one responsible for it. You hear me?"

"I am not blaming myself for his mindset or his deeds. Of course, they are his and his alone. I am pained at the thought of him using all of us to hide behind his ugly truth. He used Mol the most, and I wonder if there are more casualties than we know."

He shook his head in a manner that indicated that he was still finding it hard to digest.

"I wouldn't even want to go there. This rock that is sitting on my chest is enough to crush me. In all of this, I am the one who is somewhat blameworthy and has been hanging my head in shame ever since."

Jay was someone she could bare her soul to and now that he knew, she thought it best to unburden what was weighing heavy on her soul.

"Why you, darling?" Not comprehending the significance of her role in this episode, he wondered. "Firstly, you were not the reason they got together and married. It was away from you on all accounts. Secondly, it's not like you knew that Sam would turn out to be this guy. None of us knew."

"I did," said Urvi and broke down.

"What?" More stunned by this single word than he had been the whole previous night, Jay thought he was hearing it wrong. "What do you mean you did?"

She took some time to compose herself and narrated the whole chance encounter with Sam's escapade, her initial shock and disbelief at witnessing all of it in person, her subsequent refusal to conceal it from Molina to his incessant pleading for forgiveness, promises to be true to Molina and her gullible self, trusting and giving him another chance.

When Urvi finished telling him every bit of it till the last detail, all he asked was the question, she had been asking herself past few weeks, "It wasn't your decision to make, Urvi. It should have been Molina's," he said disappointedly, "You should have let her know that truth there and then."

Urvi hung her head down and admitted, "I realized it the hard way, and I have not been able to forgive myself since."

"I hope you do let her know now." And he got up and left.

***

CHAPTER 22
THE PLAN BEGINS

It was the hardest thing Urvi ever had to do, and she felt like a serial killer who was on a murderous spree but was killing the same person again and again. She finished, and both the friends sat there motionless as if life had pressed a pause button. Molina was also emotionless at this point. The inertness must have been somehow therapeutic and must have helped in restoring the dampened spirits because as soon as Molina's phone rang and broke the stillness, she perked up a bit. She took the call in a rather welcoming tone and smiled through most of it. When she disconnected, she was wearing a very visibly pleasant smile on her.

"Good news. Absolutely fabulously good news."

She rubbed her hands in glee and said, "I am good to go."

The timing couldn't have been better for Molina and Urvi. Urvi had fallen in her own eyes and was finding it hard to face her friend after admitting her idiocy about keeping Sam's episode from Molina, and the good news just about that moment came as a respite to her. For Molina, knowing about that episode added to her resolve to go ahead with her plan and made it easier to celebrate her move. "Sorry, no champagne this time. Of course, for you, not at all and for me, I better avoid it too."

***

Sam, on his own, sorted the Sabrina chapter by making a financial arrangement needed to see the kid's life through to adulthood.

Everything was on paper and legally stamped. Sabrina was made to sign that she would have no claim of any kind on Sam or his earnings, and she was heavily compensated for that, too. Even his identity was not to be disclosed to the child without Sam's consent. To further encourage Sabrina to move on with her life, he even agreed to pay some more if she decided to get married soon and stay married. Knowing Sabrina, he was sure the day would come sooner than later.

He lost close to five months in all of this but he wanted his second innings at home to begin on a clean slate and he went along with the arrangement of living separate lives. He told himself that he had to gather the courage to find his voice in front of Molina and begin the damage control.

***

Molina had finished her morning yoga routine and was watering the plants on the kitchen window sill when he thought he saw a weird bulging stomach through her fitted yoga gear. He didn't know why, but a strange uneasiness engulfed him, and he barely managed to stagger to the chair close by. He sat there, his eyes still on the bulge, observing keenly to confirm his suspicion. But he couldn't. He chided himself for overreacting but struggled to brush it off. After a while, he put both things on hold – his reaching out to her to seek forgiveness and his conclusion of the optical illusion.

He let some more time pass, but each passing day confirmed his fear more and more. And it soon became clear.

Molina was undoubtedly pregnant.

And he had no way to know how.

***

The excruciating pain and agony that took over Sam made him somewhat lifeless, and it started reflecting on his everyday life. He was losing interest in his work, and at home, he moved around like a zombie. There were too many questions hanging loose in the air, and he had no one he could ask. The very fact that his wife was pregnant and he didn't know how and by whom was in itself beyond humiliating, and on top of that, his inability to have the power to question her crushed him. He had no one he could confide in either, so there was no available counsel or comfort. He had got the biggest blow a guy could get to his pride, and he couldn't even let it out.

Urvi herself was showing a lot more than Molina, and he calculated hers to be around the time of their visit to the gynaecologist, where they had a run-in with him and Sabrina. She was still avoiding him, and Jay was not to be heard or seen. Sam had understood that those two were openly hostile towards him, and till now, he had let them be. But he couldn't any more. They were the only common link between him and Molina and the only ones with access to their secrets. His, and now Molina's. He had to infiltrate into their surliness and warm his way back in. It was nearly impossible, but it was the only way he could regain his sanity. He also knew that cracking Urvi was crucial before even trying to go anywhere near Jay. He played a lot of different scripts in his mind to find the most suitable one, but none weighed in his favour. They came out looking staged and forced. He was on a very delicate footing, and any wrong, unsightly move on his part would throw him into deeper trouble. He had to go with an honest approach with no drama, no falsehood and no fabrication.

Sam was looking for a window of opportunity, and it arrived when Molina went on a sight visit to a nearby town where a client of hers was opening a branch of his now-growing chain of home stores. She was assigned to do the interiors on the lines of their existing stores, and she went with her team for two days to set the ball rolling. Sam was left in charge of babysitting at home. He was lucky that Urvi was a concerned aunt to his son, and by evening, she came to check on the kid. With his favourite burger, chips and a milkshake in hand, she entered with the spare house keys that she always had on her.

***

CHAPTER 23
THE PREGNANCY

Sam had heard the key turning in the door and knew it could be no one but her. He wouldn't have bothered to go up to the door to see if things were all hunky dory between them both, but that day, he could use the walk to the door to his advantage.

He almost leapt towards the entrance and caught Urvi right in his face as she stepped inside. There was no escaping him.

"Hi!" he said as politely as he could and made way for her to walk past. "Could you please be kind enough to spare a little time to talk to me?" he said from behind her.

"There is nothing left to say."

She turned and faced him. She shouldn't have. Because what she saw was the ghost of a friend who was once very dear to her. At that moment, she realized that it was never going to be easy to say no to this face. Trying very hard to resist, she said point blank, "I am here for your son, and that's all I will be here for. You and I were over the day you betrayed my trust in your promised words. We have been through this entire rigmarole once before, and I will live to regret that day. I am not the same Urvi anymore and try as you may, you will never fool this one." Her voice was not in sync with her words, and Sam saw this as a sign of a leeway.

"I put my head on a platter for you to do as you please. I am not asking for forgiveness. Mol can punish me for the rest of my days. That's what I deserve. I concede my sins, and I want to pay for them. I just want you to tell her not to completely withdraw like she has."

The helplessness and defeat in his voice were enough to tell her that the man was on the brink of collapse.

"How do you think anyone can pay for something as horrendous as this?" Her anger was fighting with her compassion, and she was left to see which would win. "How do you think someone puts back life into a corpse? Do you realize what you have killed here? Because it's Molina, she will never tell, and you will never know. But I will tell you so you know, and I will tell you that you have killed the Molina that we knew. This is not your Molina, and she will never be. That one is gone."

The high rising emotions were making her dizzy and she went and found a chair to sit on. He ran in to fetch her a glass of water.

"What you have in place of her is bothering you now, isn't it?" He heard her from behind him.

He kneeled down and handed her the glass. She drank slowly and took her time to catch her breath. She glanced at him and saw fear in his eyes mixed with surrender and felt a surge of pity but still couldn't stop herself from hurting him further, "This is your punishment. This new, unknown stranger, Molina, is your punishment. You want to get punished, right? She has you signed up for a life of punishment. And it's right there in front of your eyes, and you can't do shit about it because, my dear friend, I have you by the balls. I have your signed death certificate; I have your prenup."

"Whatever you say, Urvi. I will do whatever you and Molina say. But at least say something. She has just gone mum on me. There is just stony silence in this house. Forget about me, but she deserves some chatter, some laughter, and some sign of life. The kid deserves to. How long can we live like this?"

"Is this what is really bothering you, Sam?" she asked sarcastically.

"This too, and then there is this, you know...." He hesitated and let it hang in the air for Urvi to pick it up. But she didn't. The torture would be tenfold if he had to say it out loud, and she wanted to enjoy his anguish. She wanted the taste of sweet revenge.

This was the ultimate sweet revenge. How she wished Molina was there to witness it.

"You were saying?" Urvi teased. She couldn't let Sam save his ego and spell it out for him. He had to do it himself.

A bit of wait and Sam accepted the defeat, "How is she pregnant? How can she be pregnant? We haven't been. You know... we are."

The entire accumulated burden of past months erupted like a volcano and the once solid strong fearless man was drowning in tears.

Once again, Urvi wished that Molina had been there.

She also wished Molina was present because she didn't know how to handle this unexpected turn of events. Molina had let her into her scheme of things. She knew pretty much most of what was needed to know. They had numerous deliberations before they agreed on what Molina wanted to do as the best and right way forward. Their sole purpose was to raise a head in disapproval against this century's old injustice; let it be known that the favour can be so easily returned. Yet, do something fruitful and positive to escape regret and bitterness. The scars of infidelity could never be wiped out, but the wound could be helped to heal if the victim resolved to seek justice in any way possible and accomplished a similar dent in the heart of the wrongdoer.

It became very difficult for Urvi to fathom what Molina would have done with a weepy Sam. She wasn't even sure that Molina had seen this side of him. He was sobbing obsessively and didn't look like he was anywhere near the end of it. Not that Urvi was in a hurry for him to stop. In all fairness, this was the long-awaited moment for them, and though she had enough fun for now, she didn't make any efforts to abort it. She would need every little detail till the end when she would sit down to narrate it to Molina. When the crying ended, she picked up the conversation again.

"First, you collect yourself, go sit over there and let the insensitive bastard that you are come out. I can only talk to someone I know, and this tear-jerking performance is quite a put-off," she said sternly.

Sam pulled himself up and slumped on the couch across from her. He made another attempt at his query. "She is my wife, Urvi, and she is carrying a baby that is not mine. Do you know how it feels? Can you imagine what I am going through day in and day out, watching her prancing around the house, constantly teasing me with her ever-growing bulge?"

He was truly hurting and humiliated; anybody in his place would, but in his case, he was guilty of equally hurting. Sitting there was an accused, accusing another of the same crime he was guilty of. Expecting empathy, understanding and commiseration for his sorry state could have seemed amusing, and to console him would have been beyond awkward. Even if someone wanted to extend a supportive shoulder, he couldn't do it without feeling ridiculously bigoted or phoney. There was no defence in Sam's favour in all of this, and he may not have realized it as yet, but Urvi knew he would soon.

She secretly marveled at Molina's masterstroke.

And smiled at her victory.

An ultimate poetic justice, if there was any.

***

CHAPTER 24
A DOSE OF HIS OWN MEDICINE

Over an hour into the conversation and all Sam got to know was that Molina was indeed pregnant and to an extent, it had worked as a glue to her broken heart. It couldn't have come at a better time and Urvi was in no mood to nick her drying wounds. Urvi had not asked her any details regarding baby's possible father but Molina had admitted to her that it wasn't Sam. And then left it at that.

What an insult to injury.

Sam had been dreading this, and now he knew that Urvi knew. How many more knew, and how many more would? The public humiliation would follow him everywhere and this devastation would turn him into a joke.

His hands were tied. His mouth was sealed. He was slouching on his guilt couch and was not able to get up.

He couldn't plead his case. He didn't have a case.

***

With his house burning and his world collapsing, he forgot about his side of the family and hers, too. Where would they fit into all of it? Both families may have had their fair share of shortcomings, and one may have had more than the other, but none had such a scandalous incident in their name. Forget scandal. They didn't have as much as a dot on their social or professional name. If a finger had to be pointed at Molina's parents, it could only be in relation to them being non-achievers. Their career began and ended at the same spot, and for a society obsessed with success and riches, fame and power, they had nothing to offer.

Sam's dad was renowned in the medical field and had earned a squeaky-clean image himself for his ethics and disciplinary lifestyle. Much was expected from his offspring. Except for Sam, others tried to live up to the name and pretty much followed their father's footsteps. What would become of his parents when they'd learn that one of theirs had not only crossed the line but had gone too far? This dreadful deed of Sam would be outright unpardonable.

He was anyway losing sleep over the whole fiasco and was dodging the family get-togethers by making one excuse after another, waiting to see when Molina opened the can of worms. He was sure she would one of these days. And he was sure which side his family would take. They adored her. There were four daughters-in-law, and comparisons were inevitable. She won the first round as soon as she expressed her desire to live in the same house as them. The other two before her had shown their displeasure at sharing the living space, and this condition was put forth at the time of the wedding discussions, which was that the girls would like to live separately. This proposition had dejected Sam's parents, and they began to foresee a lonesome future ahead of them.

Then came Molina, and their world lit up. She had lived her life in an empty house for long hours, and she cherished the constant companionship of someone or another. She began bonding with her in-laws, and she and she alone became their darling. Observing her with his family, Sam also made an extra effort to be warm and caring towards her parents, and soon, the family became big and happy.

When they both started climbing the ladder of success and money started pouring in, they began planning to move into a bigger and better house. Molina made sure Sam's parents were not only consulted but were dragged everywhere they went property hunting. This gesture left a lasting imprint on their hearts about Molina's all-encompassing love for them. And though they stayed back in their own accommodation as the house Molina and Sam chose was right around the corner, they never forgot the pride of place that Molina always gave them in her life.

If and when the news reached them, he knew the doors of their home would shut on him. If that wasn't enough, Molina's heartless display of retaliation made things hellish. It was killing him to think that both the families were going to be in full-on celebratory mode, knowing there was another baby on the way for him and Molina, while Sam dreaded to be anywhere around it. He was sure he would be pulled into the festivities and would not only be expected to participate but be jubilant and blissful about it.

Only he knew that if there was anything farthest from being blissful, it was his life.

***

CHAPTER 25
THE FACADE

Sam was no different. He was free to walk away. Especially now, when clearly, he was defeated and was lying flat on the ground. He never had difficulty falling in love. In fact, he fell too often and too soon for his own good. He was young and successful; he could get his pick whenever he wanted. People end marriages, divorces happen, and life moves on. There was nothing that was stopping him from finding his self-respect and peace back. He must know that Molina was never going to love him like she did, if at all. What was he hanging on for? Molina was not the kind to fight for him to stay back. In fact, had he come clean and confessed his misadventure to her, even to the extent of admitting to the baby, she would have given him a loose rope.

She was a woman of the world and knew things happen. Love changes hands, and people outgrow it. It's not unheard of, and though she may not have imagined it ever happening to her, considering her close-to-perfect married life with him, she would have conceded to the facts at hand. If it had come to it, he could have ended it all in a civil, amicable manner, and neither would have been hurt.

But things unfolded in a very undesirable manner. It began with him being caught at the crime scene with blood on his hands and no time to clear the traces of his involvement. Whatever followed kept going against him, and he couldn't recover to find his bearings.

After a short sentencing, he was hopeful of being pardoned for good behaviour, like they show in the movies and could focus on repairing the damage.

***

Molina chose to keep her cards close to her chest. With life throwing an unexpected grenade at her and blowing her up in shreds, she didn't want to bet on any favourable outcome. She thought it best to keep her own and Sam's family out of it for the time being, as she didn't want another set of problems to cater to. She knew the impact would be horrendous on both sides, and there would be a lot of give and take of extreme emotions, angry or otherwise. And at this point in her life, she could do without any of it. The meetings with the families went on like normal, although the frequency and duration started reducing. The effort it took to keep up the pretence while mingling with people outside of themselves was unnerving and, at this point, meaningless to them, and they found innumerable excuses to stay out or at least get out early from their combined gatherings.

Sam was always on tenterhooks around his own folk, not so much as Molina's, as he was aware of their reticence and banked on a response of flight and not fight from them. His own was another story altogether. All echoed what the father felt, and he knew this act of his wasn't just going to be unacceptable, but he might just get exterminated from the family fold. His supremely vocal and condemnatory family would be so loud in tearing him to bits that their voices would follow him back home and might stay with him long enough to create havoc.

Not only did Molina know of his fear of disclosure, she used it to her advantage. Keeping mum on that front was like having an ace up her sleeves and since the game was on, she had every intention of taking it to the finish line and winning with no foul to her name.

Her parents kept dropping in like they used to, and she went the whole hog to project a happy family show. Sam was included in person or in conversations, and though the deception and sham killed her from within, she went along like a seasoned actress. She had to get used to this and master it eventually, for this was going to be her life.

The elation on both sides on learning about her pregnancy made things easier for Molina but extremely excruciating for Sam. She was happy that the focus and conversations shifted toward the arrival of their baby and that every concern and care related to that was welcome. She could do some pampering and looking after herself. Already in a fragile state of mind, she used the situation to hide behind her occasional touchiness or sulkiness, and whenever she was in a depressive mood, she pretended to be tired and exhausted and refused to leave the room. Every whim of hers was accommodated, and all this left Sam facing the front with no excuse to offer.

There clearly was a lover, or so Sam concluded and going by the way she was bravely carrying his baby, it was testimony enough that she had found someone she could love to this extent. She was way too desirable a woman, for her to struggle to find love. She just had to look around and look interested. With so much anger and hatred towards him, he was sure she didn't take much time to welcome the advances.

***

Veer in all of this, was having the best time. His dad was being unrecognisably nice and surprisingly heard the unsaid, and gave the unasked. And although Veer was too young to notice the favourable changes, unsuspectingly his spirits were getting a boost and strangely the scenario became a better ground for him to grow in, instead of being the other way round.

Neither Sam nor Veer would ever know the stabbing pain Molina had to go through to push all her emotions and subsequent actions under the rug. She was not an actress who could seamlessly and successfully pull off an act. And even if she was, this act was not an easy one to manage. But mothers are known to be donning any hat, if required, to protect their child. And Molina was no different. She was a mother, after all, and a wise, mature, intelligent and thoughtful one at that. She was not given to impulses and was not a fan of hasty decisions.

Keeping Veer's current well-being in mind was of utmost importance, and she had to put aside her personal betrayal and put it on hold as she figured out how to save them both without sacrificing anything. This involved their entire life ahead, and neither needed to pay for something that they were not guilty of. The foolproof strategy was the need of the hour, and it required time for contemplation and an ingenious approach. The task was not just about a one-time payback or penalty. It was about a life sentence. No short-term pain or quick penance. It needed a wound that never healed like hers would never. It needed a bed that kept him awake like hers had become.

Everything was to change, while nothing seemed to change, at least for Veer. That was the mission, and Molina went to work with the precision of an expert judge. What would be the befitting decree if it were presented in the court of law? And not the legal court with constitutional dictates. There, the loopholes work more in favour of the accused than the victim. There, the evidence and testimony ruled, which entirely depended on the ability to present, and the one who lied better walked away a winner.

Molina failed miserably at lying and so her path couldn't lead up to the steps of any courtroom. She had to be her own attorney, her own witness, her own evidence and her own judge. And in her own courtroom.

And she needed a favourable verdict.

She needed her pain undone.

***

CHAPTER 26
PAYBACK

Jay patiently heard Urvi's word-to-word account of her altercation with Sam, and he got this uneasy feeling that the girls were being way too malicious. Their conduct had become mean and vindictive, which was fine and even justified, but they were leaving no room for a rational approach, and lately, it had started to worry him. Knowing it was a delicate matter involving fragile emotions, he had kept his discomfort to himself. But that day, he felt responsible for taking charge and diluting the poisonous impact of their tricks. His stance was still the same, but somewhere in his heart, he feared that this unbearable blow to Sam might prove fatal and may drive him to irreversible self-harm. And if that happened, the girls would not be able to live with themselves, irrespective of everything. To save everyone from the possible calamity, he picked up the phone and called Sam. Not to support or comfort him but to balance the equation for him in the best possible way.

As mentioned before, Jay was a fair guy on all counts, and he preferred to have a balanced perspective on the occurrences in his life. His phone went unanswered; he waited for a bit and dialled again. Still no answer. After a few more attempts, he panicked, picked up his car keys and drove to Sam's house. He knew Molina was out of town, and Jay would be able to have a heart-to-heart with him. Sam was pacing up and down on the front lawn when Jay got out of his car. He heard the door slam and looked in Jay's direction. His eyes lit up like a thousand bulbs, and a ray of hope appeared on his creased face. Jay gave him a warm, friendly hug, and Sam gestured toward the inside of the house.

"Can I offer you a drink, Jay?" Sam knew that it was not a friendly visit and that Jay was there to talk about Urvi's visit. And they both could do with a drink to ride through it. Not that he had suddenly gotten very hopeful that Jay was finally there to fight his case. In fact, if anything, Jay was the last one he would bet on. They were morally two extremes, and it was unfathomable for Jay to find any justification for Sam's fuck up. Still, he was there and that too after Urvi had just given Sam an earful. It couldn't be all bad.

"Ya okay, the usual, please." With years of dining together, they knew each other's preferences.

Sam avoided sitting facing him and after handing over his drink, he sat down on the left side. People tend to turn less to their left, and Sam could do with fewer eye contacts. After what seemed like an extended silence Jay finally spoke.

"Where is it going, Sam? And I don't mean where you are taking it? You took it where you did, and that is why it stands where it does today. I just wonder where it will end. Where and when will the massacre stop?"

"I wish I knew. No one is waiting more desperately for it to end than me, but no one is more to be blamed for it than me. I am sure you can envision my position. I have lost my right to question."

He spoke in such a defeated manner that to expect any fight out of him would have been asking too much. He had surrendered to the girls just as he had to his destiny.

"That you have, and there is no undoing it," Jay said matter-of-factly. "Also, the course of action that followed was clearly aimed at paying you back and with the never-heard rate of interest. In Molina's case, at least she knows where your sin originated. With you, it will be a lifetime of ache and discomfort. You will have to live with this embarrassment and this constant reminder that you got played and how."

It was better to paint the picture in all its gore. Show the worst of worst of the coming days and then test if one has the strength and capability to sail through it. And then anything less painful than this could always come as a welcome change.

"It's understood, Jay, that all this is Molina's way of making me feel her pain. Putting me in her shoes and telling me, now walk. And I neither blame her nor am angry with her. It just pains me that this extreme step that she has taken to pass on the message may be directed at me, but it is a lifelong commitment, responsibility and beyond that, in the kid's later years, she is also answerable to that child for that decision."

"Why is it any different from your child? How is that not being irresponsible? Don't you think the same accusation should be hurled at you too?" Not one to endure the double standards, Jay called a spade a spade.

"Absolutely. In fact, I stand more accused as I betrayed her trust while she is just returning the favour. I get that. But what happened in my case was an unwanted accident and may have been a trap, now that I think of it. Not in a million years would I have wanted to introduce a child to a life of illegitimacy. It's not fair to an innocent life." Sam threw the only powerful card that he had in his hand, which he thought worked a bit in his favour. "I am really concerned here. For her and for the unborn. Whose name is she going to give the kid? Knowingly putting a child through this shameful existence is not Molina. What is she even thinking?"

"There will be two of them then, in that case. Yours and hers. Living the shameful existence." Not one to get impressed easily, Jay didn't want him to go scot-free. "And unless you decide to withdraw your name, who is to know he is not yours." Jay saw a possible threat of him disowning the kid and threw the bait. Sam saw a possible salvation and took the bait.

"Do you think I have a choice here? I am doomed any which way. If I withdraw, I will be broadcasting to the world this nightmare. I have no option but to go along, and I would happily do that if that's what gives her happiness, but it's just that knowing about some truths might make it easier to cope with. At least she has the consolation of knowing. I don't even have that," he lamented. "If there is someone, I am willing to step aside, but I should know for whom I am vacating the space. Don't you think?"

"If you are hinting at the origin of the baby, then I am sorry, but I can't help you there. I don't have any knowledge of it. You know they wouldn't part with it. And even if they did, I wouldn't divulge an ounce of it. I am sure you know that, too." Jay was blunt enough to sever that route.

"All this is so tormenting."

"It was meant to be. Don't you realize?"

"I do. Of course, I do. But I hoped that one of you would have mercy on me and see the unfairness of this ordeal." Sam was literally pleading.

"You are not in a place to make moral judgments or even be a critic. As far as this matter is concerned, your stand should be of complete understanding and support." He tried to put it on the table for him as politely as possible. No harsh words, no sermons, no mocking and no abhorrence.

Jay's peaceful, forthright approach and the fact that he made himself available at Sam's doorsteps was enough for Sam to put his trust in him. He may not have been there for support but sure enough he was there for the solution, and Sam was willing to go by his every word of advice.

"I am trying, Jay. God knows I am so trying. I admit it's not been easy for me to accept. But hanging on to that tiny little hope that even under these circumstances, if we could find a way to be anywhere close to what we were, it would be a dream."

"That's what I am here for. I would like to ask you if you even want to go through it, whatever it may be. Be warned that there will be plenty of shards floating around the house after the deluge weans, and at times, it won't be pretty." He hesitated but thought it best to put the whole picture out there. "You will end up bringing up someone else's child while disowning one of your own. The resentment may sit in as time goes by and might reflect in your actions and behaviour. You might not like what you will become. I have known you as the ever-loving, big-hearted, fun guy. You will not meet that one; we all will not get to meet that one. You may not realize it now, but it might kill you like slow poison."

Someone had to tell him, and Jay hated that it was he, but he had made up his mind not to be a bystander. So there he was.

"To be honest, I haven't thought that far. Maybe I don't want to. I just want my today to be fine and then the same for tomorrow and so on." His mindset was like that of a daily-wage guy who was content with the day's earnings to survive each day, who is physically and mentally not equipped for the long run and has resigned to a meagre existence. "Now that you are walking me through what is ahead of me, I can't see what I will be when I actually walk that road," he said honestly.

"Then I suggest, you should take your time. Think and rethink. Mull over everything I said and when and if you are ready and prepared, we can sit again and see how to take it forward. Till then take care of yourself and gather as much strength as you can, because my friend, you will need all of it and more."

He got up and nodded at Sam. A gesture that said, I hope you got it.

"I will keep everything you said in mind," said Sam as if reading his mind. "And thanks, Jay. You being here like this, despite everything. You don't know what it means to me. I don't think I can ever thank you enough."

"In my eyes, you have earned this visit. The reason I am here is because irrespective of what you did, which for me is unpardonable, there is something else you did that made me take a step back and see you in a different light. And you know what that is? Your acknowledgement of the misconduct, your subsequent repentance and your willingness to accept any form of punishment. It's rare and, for me, unheard of. Men commit this brutality so frequently and then either deny it without batting an eyelid or make it worse by defending it. They shrug it off as something regular and inevitable. Something that women should learn to live happily with. But you gave Molina the right to get hurt, and you opened yourself to every possible atonement." Jay patted him on his heart and said, "It's not all black in there, and that says a lot about you."

Their eyes met, and there were tears in both.

***

CHAPTER 27
SOME RESPITE

Urvi was waiting in the living room as Jay walked in. It was past midnight, and she looked worried. Jay had left in a rush, and she had no idea where to go. She had an inkling to where he could have been but avoided asking him. He would tell her on his own. There were no secrets between them, and she was okay with waiting. She didn't have to.

"I went to Sam. I am sorry, but I had to."

He went and sat next to her, removed his shoes, stretched his legs on the lounger, adjusted the cushions behind his back and narrated the whole conversation.

He assured that he still maintained his firm disapproval of the deplorable act and that his reluctance to give Sam any leeway would have been in place had Sam continued to be the jerk that he was. However, that day, Sam was a reforming offender, and he may not deserve an acquittal, but his sentence could be reduced on the grounds of good behaviour. He rationally explained how Sam's manner following the incident was that of a remorseful and apologetic person and not of someone who would shift the blame to appear faultless. He has been patient in his insult and gracious in his injury. Most turn their backs on their misdemeanours, which he didn't, and Jay thought it was commendable.

"I want you to know that I am coming from a place of humanitarian thinking. His was a punishable act, and there are no two ways about it. But I think we have covered that plenty in our previous discussions. You guys have made sure that he never stops getting punished, and it has also been immaculately attained. But the question is, what now? She clearly hasn't thrown him out, which, in my opinion, she should have. She hasn't bothered to leave him also. Fine. He pained her. She pained him back. Is there an end to the inflictions? Or is there more coming?" Jay's tone was filled with emotional fatigue, pleading for an end to the revenge saga.

It was the first time that someone spoke about Sam in all of this. Especially the integrity with which he was handling the consequences of his actions and his dignified silence. As she sat there swallowing Jay's words, she recognized the source of uneasiness she had been experiencing all this while. Maybe some part of her was picking up the signs that it was not all black about Sam, and the equilibrium of the hurt was almost indistinguishable. She had been seeing it but had not accepted it. And now she did.

And wished Molina would, too.

***

A personality like Molina's was rare if how she dealt with the most horrific episode of her life was any indication. She was not of a destructive nature. She was not given to impulsive judgments. She didn't harbour hatred or jealousy and seldom overreacted to an adverse situation. The owner of a secure, mature, wise temperament, she had to have reasoning for everything. Whether her conduct or others, whether her reactions or others, it had to make sense to her. Justification is what she sought, and then understanding of it, but never an excuse. That was a no-no.

And based on that, she did try to find any justification for the nightmare she was dragged into. She found none. All she found was a display of greed for more, where even the best was never enough.

She had seen it all around, and then she saw it in her own home.

The never-ending greed of humans.

And she was not okay with it.

***

When Urvi put forward her reassessment of the present setting, Molina heard her very patiently. She let her finish and then gave herself a lot of time to ponder over the various aspects of this interpretation. She believed in seeking correction for every action and reaction, and she was always receptive when it came to her. And coming from Urvi carried a lot more weight. It could be the same person they were talking about, but they had different equations with him. She may agree with their argument, and she did, but they were mere witnesses while she was the casualty. And if anyone needs to get stitched up, it would be her.

"I agree with everything that Jay said. It's all there in front of us. I won't deny that I do see the efforts to reverse the damage. The eagerness and sincerity are also not lost on me. And I recognize that it's commendable given my open demonstration and rejection of him." She jestingly pointed at her tummy and winked at Urvi.

How far had she come? And wonder where she was heading. Urvi looked at her friend, who once couldn't even hurt a fly.

"But?" Urvi could see a but following.

"Haha. Smart. Huh?" She caught on Urvi's alertness and impatience.

"There is not so much a 'but' as there is a 'why'. Even if I open my arms to the amended version, the conscience will always have a 'why' written all over it and that too in bold letters. 'Why' did he do it? Give me one good logical, sensible justification for it, and I will write that one 'why' off. It's a man thing, or it's what most men do, but it is not an answer. Not for me. And then the other 'why' is, why am I expected to live with it? I know, there again, the majority vote will go against me. But I want my this 'why' to be answered too." She displayed no anger, no bitterness and no spite, just plain lucidity.

"There is no answer to these 'whys'. There never will be. And that's not what we are solving here. Because we can't, no one can. It's a lone battle, and each one fights in the best possible way."

"Exactly. And this is my way. Should I be questioned? Really?"

"No, you shouldn't, no way. And no one is questioning you here."

"Then what is this? You and I always agree on a simple solution. One needs something outside the marriage; one should stay outside the marriage. Have balls. Walk out. That's legal. That's human. That's honest. Why this foul play? Nah… it's slaughter. It's butchery. It's that bad."

She looked away as if visualising the bloodshed. Only someone who bled like her would know what she was picturing.

"For whatever reason, this one human misstep is looked at as a weakness, and though reluctantly and with shattered hearts, it is overlooked or even pardoned. I can feel that in the long run, it will hang over my head like an invisible sword, ready to drop with its sharp edges and cut me into pieces." She put her fears out.

"If that's what you dread, then go with your gut. I have been with you on this from day one. You know that. You can take your life in any direction, especially when the co-pilot steered away on his own. We are afraid, Jay and me, I mean, and that the turbulence shouldn't get so harsh that the crash is inevitable. In simple terms, we don't want you to reach a point where the penalty becomes more brutal than the offence." Urvi finally said what she had gone there to say. "By your own logic, even you can walk out. It doesn't have to be an eye for an eye."

"For me, it has to be. If I have a distorted vision, you do too. I understand your concern, and I understand that it comes from an unbiased and empathetic place. So, no sweat, darling. Keep faith. Keep trust. I am in safe hands."

There was no one way to heal. Every heart would find its own way. Hope Molina's way succeeded.

***

Jay's approval of Sam's efforts and the understanding of his ordeal gave a boost to his fading spirit and somewhat lifted his morals. It was like the power of a healing hand. It also made the everyday affliction a little less, as Jay's rational explanation of the similarity helped him to see things differently. Every time he saw Molina with the baby bump, her staring at Sabrina at the clinic flashed before him, and his self-reproach overthrew his pain. And over a period of time, out of guilt, he began to relax around it, though not yet accepting it fully. He kept his eyes alert for any hint or clue of an ongoing affair, but either Molina was being overtly smart and cautious, or he was not good at this game. The mystery of whose baby still hovered over his head, and he knew he wouldn't ever be able to get rid of it. It was Molina's punch on his face, and the imprint was there to stay.

Since he couldn't find no suspicious man lurking in and around Molina, the fear of dealing with a potential lover slowly stated diminishing and towards the end of the pregnancy he was convinced that Molina was on her own in this, just like Sabrina was left to be. There was no one, not any more, at least. He then began attributing it to a night of revenge. He somehow managed to seek some comfort in that.

Molina began to loosen up a little, too. Maybe consciously or subconsciously, the effect of Urvi's counsel made a way into her demeanour.

***

CHAPTER 28
THE GETAWAY

In all of this, Urvi's pregnancy got sidelined, and Molina felt a tinge of selfishness. She wasn't being fair to her friend, who was going to be welcoming a child of her own after years of waiting. She decided to surprise her by hosting a baby shower for Urvi, and she got busy planning it. Molina hired a professional hand to source and arrange the nitty gritty, and since it was meant to be a surprise, she ended up keeping a lot of things from Urvi. Who, in turn, didn't understand when she caught Molina's few lies. It mostly had to do with her whereabouts, and it seemed bizarre. They had no secrets between them ever. None were required.

It started with dodging the questions, then lying, and then outright refusal to reply. They would banter over one unexplained outing, then another but nothing would come out of it. It became a little frustrating as it went on, and then got annoying and then plain suspicious. When persistent pestering and subtle threats of a possible fallout between them also didn't help, Urvi took it to the ultimate conclusion. Molina was definitely hiding something.

Or was she hiding someone?

Urvi had two options. To ignore and turn the other way or go the whole hog and get down to confront her. She would have to determine whether it was even right to interfere in Molina's personal space, especially if she was not in the mood to share. She had taken a terrible jolt to her self-respect and been through a lot of heartache. Whatever it was, if it was helping her in any way, why should Urvi stir the pot? She should wait and watch.

There were phone calls that flashed on her phone with just initials and kind of compelled her to step out to receive them. Her tone turned hushed as she spoke to a particular caller, and when she couldn't walk off, she was seen rejecting the call. The increasing secrecy didn't go down well, and soon, Urvi decided to get to the bottom of it. What if Molina was heading toward a bigger disaster? What if she was being misled, exploited or manipulated? She was hurt and vulnerable. She might be suffering from low self-esteem and rejection. That was an easy target. The perfect playground for a crook.

After a night of nightmarish thoughts, Urvi landed up at her workplace one early afternoon. Partly to satisfy her increasing concern about the goings-on and partly to find a truce to the recent upheaval in their equation. The door to Molina's cabin was locked from inside. Urvi was told to wait. And it was. A moment of déjà vu.

The day she sat outside a locked room while Sam was having a day of sinful fun inside.

Was Molina going all out as payback? She told Molina about her catching Sam red-handed. Has she been waiting to get back in every possible way? Her brain was getting foggy now, so she closed her eyes and began breathing deeply to calm her nerves. She was there to rescue her friend from a further fall if there was any coming. She couldn't afford to lose her strength. The door opened, and to make matters worse, out came a strikingly handsome young man.

***

Finally, it dawned on Urvi that she wasn't as required to rebuild Molina as she had taken responsibility for. Did she get involved more than needed, and in the bargain, had she put her life and its celebration on hold? Her own life replayed in front of her, and she felt a sudden sense of loss for the time wasted. And worst of all, she had forgotten to enjoy and make memories of the most meaningful experience of her life. She forgot to enjoy her pregnancy, get pampered, and remember that this was once in a lifetime. She had put her entire life in the back seat to be available for Molina and to nurse her wound. She was aware that it all originated from her genuine affection and concern for her, but she was also aware that her over-involvement was somewhere a result of her underlying guilt about withholding Sam's flaw. Like a trusting and humanitarian person, she had given Sam a second chance. She would have to stop holding herself responsible any longer.

***

The day she ventured into Molina's office and came face to face with the stranger walking out of her locked cabin, she felt a bit awkward but somehow managed to put on a relaxed demeanour. She had chatted warmly with Molina, displaying no shock, inquisitiveness, discomfort, or disapproval. Nothing was mentioned about the past week or the present day. She had offered the done-to-death, a most convenient lie that had stopped convincing anyone from generations that she was in the neighbourhood. Of course, she knew Molina had not bought it, but she didn't care. Everyone around her was lying. Everyone was hiding and fooling without care and getting away with it, too. All this left Urvi disillusioned and disbelieving. She started staying alert even around her own husband and paying more attention to every word and action of his.

Jay mistook her sudden overt attentiveness and availability as her appreciation for his merits and it made him keener to prove his worth. In the bargain their own home benefitted and the couple got more time together. With Molina slipping down on her priority list, Urvi diverted her time and attention to her soon to arrive baby and Jay finally found his home in a celebratory mood.

He offered a small getaway and Urvi jumped at the offer. A quiet secluded beach was agreed upon and after a superfast planning and booking, Urvi and Jay set off for their much-deserved break.

In her attempt to stay clear of Molina's personal space, Urvi forgot to inform Molina about her trip. And unfortunately, it collided with Molina's surprise baby shower for Urvi. For the day of the bash, Molina had instructed an associate from their NGO to call Urvi just a night before for fear of any disclosure. She was just to inform Urvi that since Molina was occupied with another engagement, she would need to attend the felicitation of one of their artists. When the call was put through to Urvi to get her ready for the surprise, she had just checked into her hotel room after a day of taxing travel. She had put her phone on mute and didn't check it till well after unpacking and showering. She had picked up her phone for the time when she found four missed calls from her office. Food was ordered from room service, and she was waiting as she put on her nightclothes. Not wanting the food to get cold, she sat down to have her dinner with her husband. Away from the turmoil and weariness of the past few months combined with daylong travel and her pregnant state, she finished her dinner and curled up in bed. The phone call was forgotten.

Molina's night went tossing over the unanswered call, and she woke up with a sinking feeling that she was heading for a debacle concerning the day's do. There were eighteen missed calls on her phone, a lot more than on Urvi's, and the timeline covered most of the night. She dialled back the number, and an extremely shaky voice answered.

"Hello, ma'am," she heard.

"Hello, what happened? So many missed calls? All okay?" she asked but knew the reply.

"Ma'am, I just spoke to Urvi, ma'am. She is in Maldives on vacation. And she is not sure of her return. She says her husband has booked only one way, and they would take a call as they go along."

Silence. There was no more information to impart, yet both held on to the phone as if holding on to hope.

"Sorry, ma'am, what should we do about the preparations?" After a long wait, the shaky voice asked.

"Let the decoration be as it is. Please call the guests and inform them that the party has been postponed. We will call them as soon as the next date is fixed."

She took good care to hide her disappointment in her voice and said enthusiastically, "As for the food, let the staff continue with the treat. The remaining food can go to the kids. Take the balloons too and distribute them as well." Whatever good can come out of it, she thought.

For the baby shower, she would rearrange the food and balloons. She had the rest of the paraphernalia. The only thing needed was Urvi's return. And this time, she would make sure there was no glitch.

***

Urvi and Jay went all out to utilize their time together as they knew soon the baby would arrive, snatching all their time, attention and energy. And they would have very little left for each other. Urvi kept thanking Jay for suggesting the break; she didn't know how badly she needed it. Jay was happy she agreed, given how far ahead she was in her pregnancy. Finally, she got the prerequisite pampering and indulging that she heard women demand and receive. Jay went all out to arrange an exotic massage for her and organized cozy romantic dinners. After one such dinner, they decided to take a walk on the well-lit beach along the seaside restaurant, reminiscing the last few months and the unbelievable strain it had put on their own life when suddenly Urvi stopped in her tracks.

It was what Jay said that made her see the entire aftermath in a new light. How did she forget something so useful?

"You know, all said and done, it's still laudable the way Sam had conducted himself with so much poise and grace. I must admit, I never thought he had it in him to bow down to anyone and anything, no matter how wrong he had been. I had a very different impression of him. I liked him, I won't deny. You just can't 'not' like him. But there is something about him that always told me that he is not someone who is given to surrender. Not even if you put a gun to his head." As soon as Jay said that, Urvi flashed back to the gun she once had to his head.

It was so long ago. She neither had the desire to keep the memory alive nor did she feel the need to. Remembering it meant that she anticipated its usefulness somewhere in the future. She thought acquiring it meant never having to need it. She had forgotten about it, but had Sam? Maybe Sam didn't because of his mammoth progress and enormous wealth. The gun may have become more potent and hazardous for him. She would have to find out. She would have to test him. She would have to flash the gun yet again.

She would have to read the prenup. Out loud.

***

Urvi didn't know what Molina's reaction would be when she learned about the prenup. Something that should have taken place only between herself and her husband, if at all, was discussed, agreed upon, and signed by Urvi and Molina's husband without her knowledge. Now, when Urvi thought about it, the significance and requirement of the agreement were not as much a problem as the people who took it upon themselves to take charge of the future repercussions in which the absentee should have been the deciding factor and by all means a consent giver.

Another grave blunder and another confession.

***

When they reached their hotel room at night, Urvi studied Jay's mood. Since he was the only one drinking, he had finished most of the wine bottle by himself. He seemed extremely pleased and in a lighter mood. He was humming as he changed. Urvi waited for him to settle in bed. She felt bad that she was about to kill the joy of a perfect evening and ruin the one chance that Jay had to live his life for what it was, without bother or guilt. Wasn't he as important to Urvi as Molina? Or maybe more, as his life only revolved around home and hearth while Molina was busy extending her horizon all this time. Sitting there contemplating, she chose her priority.

She would wait. She should.

Upon waking up, Jay saw Urvi a little less perked and took it for exhaustion. He became anxious about her health and suggested a day in.

"You really, really look pale, sweetheart. I think a bit of rest will do you good. It's going to be breakfast in bed. I can also use a day tucked in with lunch in front of the TV and dinner on the balcony. A perfect relaxing day with no agenda and no activity. What say?"

"I don't feel as bad as I look." She smiled, "But I am game to stay in and chill. I think it's the heat that got me down a bit. So, don't you worry. I will be in full bloom in no time."

"That's my girl. But promise me you won't try to be unreasonably heroic and drag any discomfort more than it needs to. If you feel we better be on our way home, I will get packing at once. You just say the word."

"Let me go through the day, and let's take a call by the end of it. If we need to be home sooner than later." Urvi grabbed the option of returning. Of course, she didn't want to spoil it for Jay and had put the thought on hold, but it had agitated the tranquillity of her stay. She knew it wouldn't be long before Jay would notice.

The day went by in a leisurely fashion. They played cards and squabbled while losing, took a nap post lunch, teased each other while attempting cross and zero at tea time and sat in bed watching a movie till late evening. Having dinner on the balcony, Jay was having his wine and was looking pensively at the endless darkness of the outstretched sea in front of them.

Urvi waited till they were tucked in bed. Resting her head on his shoulder, she suggested softly, "Let's go back."

***

CHAPTER 29
CELEBRATING URVI

Molina was desperately tracking Urvi's return, and as soon as she found out Urvi was flying in that same evening, she got rolling. Everything was back in its place in a couple of hours. Guests were pleaded to accommodate the last-minute invite, to which most agreed. They were in the loop of the failed surprise, so no one resisted. Caterers were kept on hold, with every instruction till the last detail and just had to spring into action. The full staff was in attendance, and Molina was at a salon getting her hair done. The only thing she was still working on was how to get Urvi to the venue and, more than that, how to make her come dressed for the occasion. Flying back from a leisure holiday, one is most casual and unkempt, and Molina couldn't take any chances. She would have to message her, and she did. It read.

'Sorry for disturbing you during your break, but I am told you are already on your way back. Got a new upcoming artist, and there is someone ready to sponsor the entire journey till the finish line. Will need you with me. Please dress accordingly. Will have you picked up from the airport to bring you directly. Sorry once again for ambushing you like this.'

And pressed 'sent'.

***

Urvi read the message, and though she was looking forward to going straight home, she preferred this reroute. She wanted to ease out whatever little discomfort was felt by both of them in the past few days. Molina extending an olive branch, even professionally, was welcome. She quickly opened her packed suitcase, removed whatever she could find, and changed into it. A little touch-up to her face and hair made her ready to board the flight back home.

Jay had been separately requested to accompany and was let into the secret. He took out a dinner jacket and put it in his hand carry.

'Will be happy to be there.'

Sent.

And put the phone back in her purse. There was no need for her to look into it for anything else. Her darling husband was sitting next to her, and her best friend was waiting for her. Nothing more was needed. Life was good.

***

The surprise elated her to dizziness. Overwhelmed with the euphoria, she was shaking for the first half an hour or so. She walked around, thanking with nervous energy, and her voice choked as she spoke. Molina was unsure whether it was a good idea after all, as Urvi seemed to be unable to collect herself. She almost thought of abandoning the speech that she had prepared, fearing a further collapse. She put on the screen an AV of Urvi's entire life journey and watched as Urvi wept and wept. By the end of it, she appeared to have become lighter and a lot more stable.

Molina clicked the glass in a typical filmy manner. She had gone all out filmy for her drama queen and left nothing to desire. It was once in a lifetime, and it had to be perfect. She clicked the glass, and expectantly, everyone fell silent. Molina took the cordless mic in her hand and began.

"Let me begin by thanking all of you for making it here, in spite of the very forceful last-minute invite, and I'm sorry for cancelling the earlier date." She glanced at an astounded Urvi and winked. "We all are as much celebrating our dearest Urvi, stepping into motherhood, as we are celebrating her presence in our lives. Needless to say, she is the only longest-lasting love of my life, and I can't even imagine my life without her ever. She picked me up at an age when no one even noticed me. She tied herself to me when I was hanging by a thread, and she put all her hopes on me when there was no hope in or around me. Whatever I became after she chose me, it's all thanks to her. I can't think of a good enough reason why her eyes rested on me out of the rest, but do I thank God that they did? Hell, yes… every single day. And I would like to continue to thank her for the rest of my life. So here is a toast to the best mother ever that's going to be out there and to the best baby ever in the world."

She raised her glass and just took a tiny sip.

"And now done with mush, let me bring the real Urvi that I am celebrating. I am celebrating a woman who has the strength to stand by what she believes no matter who it's in favour of or who it is against. Still, she is open to different interpretations if offered and has the heart to stand corrected if needed. I can't say that about anyone I know. She practices what she preaches, another thing rarely seen. But above all, she loves like no one can. Sincerely, selflessly, compassionately and completely. And in return, I hope I have been able to love her half as much."

She blew a kiss at Urvi and heard her yelling, "You have, and you have. Double, triple of that."

"And as for her flaws, well, we will need more time than a single evening. So until next time." And she sat back down amidst roaring applause and laughter.

Not one to let go of the opportunity to appreciate and thank, Urvi called for the mic and got up.

"This is by far Molina's sweetest gesture ever, out of hundreds of them that she had bestowed on me. It has left me speechless, but here I am still trying to give a speech." She laughed.

"Perhaps because I am used to riding through the abundance of surprised pleasantries thrown at me by Molina plenty of times a day. That aside, I just want to answer her question about why little me would pick a girl from a corner and guide her to centre stage; well… very few of us have an eye that can spot perfection. And I certainly started young."

She chuckled. "To my dearest Molina, I am enormously pleased to know that I am so highly appreciated and valued. Don't mind hearing it more often. In fact, I would love it if you could make it a habit. If you look back, you will also admire my foresight, as eventually, your gains became mine, and I have been reaping the benefits ever since! So a toast to me too, the youngest talent hunter ever."

And she could hear the crowd cheering and whistling. "You took me to all the heights that life took you to, which I couldn't claim to have ever done on my own. But what I can promise you is that I am with you during all your highs and all your lows, and no matter what or where, you will always be my priority. Along with Jay, my hubby dearest."

She quickly added, "To Molina and to Jay, without whom there wouldn't have been a cause for this celebration," she jested and sat down.

***

The evening had left a permanent grin on her face, and she had been going on and on about how lucky she was to be loved so dearly. This gesture had elevated Molina even more in her eyes. She was so wrong in feeling that her life was getting sidelined in lieu of Molina's, never realizing how Molina was doing her best to make it all about Urvi and her happiness. Getting finally introduced to Molina's suspected lover as the event planner made her guiltier, and her resolve to test Sam became stronger. The real intention behind Sam's changed tune needed to be looked into, and this time, the vulnerable, soft Urvi was going to stay home while the shrewd, alert one would step out for the job.

After months, Jay and Urvi had a night that felt like a massive celebration. Back from a fulfilling holiday and welcomed by an act of immeasurable love and pampering, the couple went to bed full of gratitude and slept like never before.

***

CHAPTER 30
THE PRENUP

Urvi decided to meet Sam all by herself, throw the agreement in his face and study his response. She could be very observant if she wanted and was quick at picking tricks. She was going to be facing a verified wrongdoer, who had misled her a couple of times and so this time she was going to be extra cautious and wouldn't let him con her.

He was at the far end of the café with his back to the entrance as if hiding from the rest of the world. He was busy looking down and fidgeting with something. When she reached the table, she found his copy of the prenup spread out in front of him.

He beat her to that, too.

"It has been on my mind for long, but I didn't know where any of us were going and what was required of me." He flipped the pages and removed something that looked like a legal document. He pushed it towards Urvi and said, "Here, all that I own and all that I promised. Every single word that I gave you is delivered here. You can go through it at your convenience, and if there is anything that is missed or not fulfilled, you know whom to call." Saying that, he got up and left.

All her rehearsed strategy and consequent conclusion went for a toss as he left her stunned with the most unimaginable comeback. Not in her wildest dream did she think that he himself would throw on her face what was supposed to be her weapon and her trump card. Why did he do it? What made him stick his neck out? Was there anything in her tone that gave away her discontent? That can't be. These papers must have been in the process of getting ready for some time, and she made the call just that morning. Then what prompted or forced him? Guess she'd never know, she conceded.

Only if she was as smart as she thought.

The masterstroke was going to, at last, win Sam his seat at the table and was to help clean a lot of dirt off his being. What was to stay buried were the facts that it was his smart move to try to save his entire life savings from a claim by someone who, now, he wasn't even sure was his child. Lately, Sam has been getting feedback that Sabrina has someone other than him in her life around the time he hooked up with her. And apparently, even that guy was made to believe that the child could be his. Sam was trying to get to the bottom of it and find out if even the other guy was asked to compensate financially. He would take a call on withdrawing the monetary arrangement once he was certain about the identity of the child's father, but till then, his hard-earned money had to be secured. He wasn't going to lose his wealth to a con woman.

Already feeling rotten about throwing caution to the wind and falling into the trap of a gold digger seductress, the revelation of the possibility of her scamming him angered him so much that he hurriedly relocated his funds to Molina.

He forgot that by putting everything in Molina's name so that one day his son would have the claim over it, he was also allowing Molina's illegitimate unborn child to have the same.

By the time it struck him, it was too late.

***

Again, at the emotional crossroads, Urvi was tearing her hair in frustration when the same thought entered her mind. Man, just put a bigger noose around his neck. He had not just opened a bottle of champagne and celebrated his wife and her lover by providing a cushy and affluent life to their baby, but he had also served caviar along with the champagne by dividing his son's share in it by half.

Sam couldn't have had it worse.

The lesson he learned was that it was better not to break than to try and mend, as the few tiny pieces that splatter in the process are impossible to collect and put back in their rightful place.

Like they say, the damage had been done.

In his case, it it certainly had been.

***

Sam had gone to great lengths to do the overnight reassigning without involving Molina, and his contacts had come in very handy in making it seamless. To rush is to ruin, and since he was in no position to ask, demand or interfere, he concentrated on improving his profile at home. He became a handyman around the house, a babysitter, a tuition teacher, a chauffeur to the son and occasionally even a chef. In normal households, he would have come across as the dream husband and father, but with his resume having a big red mark, he never reached that status and was just a little bit more tolerated. It was getting more and more tiring by the day, and though he kept his head low and in control, sometimes he would reach the point of exploding. So far, he was proud that he managed his frustration well.

It came as a jolt to Molina when Sam put the details of his recompense in black and white, especially when it was put forth to her as his self-inflicted sentence to himself. She keenly checked and rechecked to digest the magnitude of this move but failed to. It was never about his money. It was never about getting reimbursed for the pain inflicted, dreams shattered, and spirit killed. There was no price tag to it, and she didn't remember ever giving any indication in that direction. The fight was all about her worth, self-respect, integrity, justice and, above all, equality. Infidelity, in her eyes, was a violation of commitment and trust and only qualified for punishment. And she had pronounced hers. She wasn't looking for anything more.

The brand-new thick stack of numerous documents spread out in front of her confused her and infuriated her even more. She didn't know what to make of it as it looked like a big pile of enticement and bribe, buying her honour and rectitude. A thick veil to hide the ugliness of blemishes and a cover to hide the stains. What was expected to change with this? This kickback? She felt like a corrupt officer asked to look the other way while the crook carried on. Sam was intensely analysing her. Living with her for years, he was accustomed to her controlled demeanour and well-thought responses. Lately, she had mastered the art of a poker face even more. Tired of waiting to see any signs and not succeeding, he braved it.

"I know it doesn't mean anything to you, and I also am aware that it doesn't make my mistake any less despicable, but I would like you to please consider this as a small fine that I must pay, and you deserve to receive. All that is in there..." He pointed at the papers, "It shouldn't even be mine to begin with. It should have been all yours. From day one, you have been my good luck charm, my motivation, my encouragement, my support and my anchor." Seeing her sitting patiently, he tried to reach for her hand, which was resting on the folders, "I want you to..."

"Whatever," she said and pushed away the files as she noticed the approaching hand. Then she got up and left.

Molina was surprised how the words that once delighted her, filled her with desire and hope, now seemed so empty and phoney. The voice that lifted her spirit and transported her to a dream world was sounding so wile. She felt like telling him to stop the pretence. Stop trying and stop hoping. She may have been a simple, gullible woman, but she was no one's fool. Now, nothing that was said to her would ever be considered without screening. She had installed a scanner in her brain to spot even the smallest dot of scepticism.

***

CHAPTER 31
URVI'S BABY

Urvi's baby arrived, and for a while, it seemed like everything was back to being what it was. How much a baby can heal was something none of them had fathomed. The bitterness, the abhorrence, and the vengeance were all forgotten, and all eyes were only on the baby. Every heart was only beating for her. Sam heard about it and came running to greet the newborn. He was not turned away, as was his fear. Instead, he was taken in warmly and even got to hold the baby. He stayed longer than was obligatory and did help running around fetching this or that. He paid daily visits till Urvi was discharged. During this time, no one brought his or her personal issues, and a very amiable and pleasant atmosphere became the order of the day. No one remembered inviting Sam, but no one did anything to shoo him away. And then, one day, when the traffic for the baby dispersed and just the four were left was when Sam tried one more time to get the thorn that was sticking in his throat out. He found it hard to construct a sentence that sounded casual yet managed to extract the desired information. He had to know it to stay sane, and giving up was not an option. So, he took one more shot at it.

"I don't know if Urvi told you, but I have literally given every last penny that I owned to Mols. Make sure that there is no one and that there will never be anyone to take away what is rightfully hers and Veer's. I know that's not what someone like Molina cares about. It's just my stupid way of soothing some of her pain."

He added to make an impression, "Maybe I am only trying to lessen my guilt." He was aware that Jay was the softest and most unbiased amongst them and he thrived on being reasonable and had a mind of his own. So, after spreading the sheet of being a caring and selfless husband, he trod on it with full caution.

"You know there is no dialogue happening between the two of us, at least not related to us both. For us, the reason here is Veer. And if we stay together for his sake, then there is nothing in it for her and me. I would rather set her free, or she frees herself from me, whichever way you look at it."

Still not able to come to the main point of concern, he added, "If only someone could tell me what's going on. After all, my wife is pregnant, and I have no idea how," he said and immediately regretted being so direct, knowing well that Jay was not someone who would give in to pressure.

"I think you have been through this with all of us before. It's not in our jurisdiction, as you were told time and again. Urvi and I can't hold your hand and walk you out of the ordeal. Yes, I get your state of turmoil, and I do empathise with your dilemma, but there is nothing more that I can offer." His voice had a certain finality. "All I can let you in with is that Molina is going nowhere, to no one and lover or no lover. She is here to stay with you under the same roof. If it helps."

"Perfectly understood. Just one last question, though." He took his last shot. "To get your perspective on my disarray, what would you have done if you were in my place? Any words of wisdom?"

"There is no need for any words. I could never be in your place."

***

Urvi got busy with the newborn, and Molina had to make up for her absence from work. She was away more, and when she got back home, she was too exhausted to be available for any kind of relationship repair. Her mood was definitely better, and she was more responsive to everyday exchanges, but her busy schedule kept her on her toes, and the remaining time, she was totally devoted to Veer. Molina's pregnancy was advancing, and he thought that being non-cooperative towards her might bring her into his arena, searching for an emotional anchor or a helping hand.

He didn't realize he was making it easier and more peaceful for her. His constant efforts at trying to win her back were draining her and disturbing her mental well-being. She also was getting suffocated, knowing fully well that his persistent attempts to be a close aide to her would adversely affect the culmination of her strategy. It was not like she could dodge and manoeuvre the finale at her will. She had to depend on the natural course, and the day and time were unknown to her. All she could do was wait to deliver. And all she needed was a clear field to go ahead without any shadow following her.

Sam handed her that as well.

***

Every decision we make has a future consequence, and no matter how smart or cunning we get, the outcome is not always what we aim at. Misfire, backfire, fail and flop, we have heard and said these words time and again. But who has ever acknowledged or learnt from a mistake? Even after falling flat on the face, the next move is still made with equal confidence and conviction. When Sam distanced himself from Molina, in his mind, he was pulling the carpet from under her feet. With Urvi occupied and she being vulnerable on her own, he thought she would lean on him for support. He didn't remember a day Molina had fended for herself and he saw a great advantage in the present scenario. He appeared to be unconcerned and unavailable and waited for the desired effect.

With a lot more time in hand sans constant surveillance, Molina got a free hand to venture out and about. Her whereabouts were unknown. This put a dent in his confidence and faith in reconciliation, and by this time, his mind had stopped suggesting any effort. Right after the birth of Urvi's baby, there seemed to be a glimmer of hope, but Sam's wrong foot forward took him back to where he was at the beginning of the disaster.

***

CHAPTER 32
SABRINA

Sabrina was out of favour with the money that was handed over to her and the legal settlement that prevented her from contacting any member of the family. She had no way to know how life had turned out for Sam after the disastrous encounter. She wasn't interested either. The unceremonious way she was discarded still hurt her and put a dent in her sense of power. Nevertheless, she kept her chin up and pranced around town, proclaiming that she handed over Sam to Molina after she realized she was pregnant with his child, as she couldn't live with herself if she broke a home. Of course, this piece of information never reached Molina.

There is a common belief that men are disloyal by nature and it's biologically not possible for them to stick to one woman all their lives. Their programming is such that they thrive on hunting and as per their risk-taking abilities they take a call. Either they try suppressing their needs or desires, or they give in to it. But none can claim to never want a beautiful distraction. Or so it's believed.

Then there are women who are neither victims nor hooks. They just put themselves up there with the men in terms of their needs and desires. They guiltlessly and unabashedly match steps with each other. No questions were asked, and no answers were given. Morality and ethics be damned.

The not-so-noble kinds were those who were always on the lookout for rich and powerful men. Their ladder to the good life of luxury and comfort were the men who, in turn, relished the attention of the young and pretty, or both. The simple rule of engagement was give and take between youth and money, beauty and power, and none were wiser. The often-odd pair of young pretty things in the arms of men of their grandfather's age is sniggered upon more for the foolishness of the grand old daddy than the greedy young needy.

In Sabrina's case, she fell into the category of women who wanted to have it all. The arrogance, self-confidence, and a damn caring attitude of that age are hard to regulate and harder to make see sense of. She was sure the life that she wished for would fall into her lap at the snap of her finger, and all she had to do was just wake up and get going. The mirror told her she had the world at her feet, and everyone else's voice was muted. The youth is anyway deaf and blind, rebellious and rash, and in her case, the endorsement of her superiority, purely on the basis of her looks, made her even more senseless and reckless. She kept picking whatever and whomever she fancied till Sam dropped her like a hot brick. Life taught her that 'it' was the actual boss, and everyone was eventually at its mercy.

Her youth was still on her side and looks, too, so the hesitancy to accept defeat and reluctance for remorse made it difficult for her to give up on her ambition and easier for her to continue with her half-baked life. Shunned by Sam, she began playing up to other probable suitors and, in the interim, found not one but three interested parties. It looked like she had moved on till one day, she spotted fully pregnant Molina. It was like tables were turned, and just like once, her pregnancy had mocked Molina in full daylight; today, it was she who was being mocked. She suddenly got that horrible feeling of being used and discarded, insulted and abandoned. The sight of a heavily pregnant Molina made it clear to her that not very long after she was forsaken by Sam, he picked up the pieces of his broken home and put them back together and how. It was as if nothing untowardly happened, and life was all good. When there are two hands that hold the murder weapon, one is not supposed to go scot-free. If he does, then the other one is left feeling resentful and often vengeful.

Sabrina felt both, or maybe a lot more.

She toyed with the idea of approaching Molina and giving her the gory details of her lustful past with Sam, but she decided against it. Clearly, Sam had done a fairly good job at damage control for her to agree to bear his child so soon after the debacle. Not throwing him out was understandable given the fact that they had a son together, and as most parents, they would have put his interests above their own. But allowing him in her bed like nothing happened needed some special talent, and she wondered what that could be. Since Molina was not the doormat type, nor was she financially dependent on him to let him walk all over her, it intrigued her what it was that did the trick.

She decided to find out. She didn't need to if she knew the truth.

***

Absolutely beaten and withered, Sam's life saw no sign of picking up. Professionally, he managed everything right, as work was where he always shone. At least there he could defeat. He told himself that his work was the only place where he couldn't mess up. But socially, he couldn't bring himself to pretend. His ego and pride had taken a severe beating though no one knew, he was sure that no one would. Still, his morals and his spirits were too worn out. It had made him a recluse. With just his son Veer for the occasional company and no other soul to comfort him at home, his adult life had become barren and empty, and he had started leaning towards severe depression.

In this state of turmoil and torture, he had to face a visitor in Sabrina. Had she come to lament the devastating effect of his absence from her life? Or had she come to seek his love and affection back? It might have been a balm to his soul, rain on his parched heart if she had. But instead, she came to him dressed to the hilt, looking every bit a woman who had the world at her feet. She flashed a humongous ring at him (which he wasn't alert enough to notice was obviously fake), threw an invented name at him as her fiancé, and went on painting a perfect picture of her life. She also made it clear that she was here not to pine for him as he was nothing more than a bad dream for her now. She had come to him to let him know that after seeing his wife pregnant with a child, she was completely free from any guilt from their fiasco. He had succeeded in putting a stamp on her suspicion that he, after all, was a rogue. She hoped that his expertise in shamelessly jumping beds with foolishly gullible women like herself and many more before her would not go unpunished. He might feel like a victorious guy right now, but not for too long. If this much wasn't enough, she proceeded to insult him further by spewing some more venom.

"Was it straight-out violent rape? Because no woman, in her right mind, would want to touch a guy like you, let alone consent to bear him a child. How did you manage this scam?"

Unable to keep her curiosity she looked at him keenly to read the words that weren't coming out. Sam was quiet as a mouse, his face seemed dead to the world and his eyes were internally shut. Nothing that she had assumed about his life now matched with his exterior. There was no mirth around the corner of his mouth, no twinkle in his eyes of a victor, no lifted head of a winner. What was there was a corpse lying on the battlefield, defeated and dead.

It didn't take long for Sabrina to get to the truth. She didn't need to prod further to get her answer. The look on his face said it all. He wasn't the cat who got his cream. He wasn't the Casanova who tramped over swooning beauties and came out looking glamorous and glorious. She didn't need to worry; she didn't need to seek revenge. She got her closure just by looking at his sorry state. But not one to let go of an opportunity, she spelt it out for him the way she saw it.

"Or maybe no miracle happened, and maybe you just got served the same unsavoury dish you had been serving. Maybe today's woman beat you to it. Maybe, just maybe, it's all fair in the end!" was her parting shot and she was gone.

***

It was the last straw that broke the camel's back. The woman who had spelt doom for him came in and stabbed his already tattered self even further. He had found relief in the thought that he was the one who had gotten rid of her and that just as his charisma and success had lured her to him, his money and mind had put her back in her place. That was where he derived his comfort from.

Somewhere, he was also today's man. And the truth was not lost on him; any woman in place of Molina would have been as hurtful and unforgiving, if not more. He knew women. He grew up around them, and he watched them. He was also a lawyer, and in his professional experience, he had seen too much viciousness and spitefulness to believe or expect anything otherwise. Women had gone to great lengths as far as mudslinging and washing dirty linen in public was concerned, and their accusations, real or concocted, had ended up stripping quite a few men of their hard-earned standing, professional or otherwise. His was a major misconduct, and the fact that she didn't make it a public trial and conducted with utmost dignity and class made him more remorseful and responsible. He was thankful that she kept a face outside of them and even spared their son from the ugliness of the incident. She had swallowed the bitter pill all on her own and never let it show on her.

He was aware that there couldn't be another Molina. He couldn't get so lucky twice in this same life.

But this Sabrina was another story. She came from a place of no significance, and her sudden appearance today at his office jolted him. He didn't anticipate that the girl he thought was disposable would end up at his doorstep and throw all the trash at him and some more. She would dare to flaunt her success story despite his rejection and mock him for his failed one, and she would leave him with the piercing unspoken truth that even he didn't have the heart to admit to himself.

Had he ever been a happy man? He tried to think but had no memory of any such feeling.

***

CHAPTER 33
REVENGE IS BEST SERVED COLD

A couple of months passed, and he settled in with the gloom and doom that his life had become till the day came when Molina didn't return home for a few days. He knew Molina was close to her delivery, and since none of his strategies were bearing any fruits, he went on to concentrate on how he would like to find comfort in his own house, along with his own family, with the changed complexities. Never in his wildest dream had he thought that his loving and devoted wife, or for that matter, any loving and devoted wife, could plan revenge of this scale and successfully execute it, too. He never took Molina to be a vengeful person who was capable of something that was so far unheard of. Who goes out and has someone else's baby and throws it in her husband's face, all the while staying in his house as his wife? Just to spite, who goes and bears any Tom, Dick or Harry's baby? Making a deliberate choice to suffer immeasurable responsibilities, financial and otherwise, and get punished just so you could punish the other? It was insane. And Molina was anything but insane.

He felt like the only man in the world who was facing something so bizarre.

And he probably was.

Molina's unknown whereabouts for days finally made him sit up. He wondered whether she had disappeared permanently after subjecting him to nine months of anguish or if she was going to return to cause a lot more of it. Was he left in a lurch, or soon his tormenter was to arrive swinging in his wife's arms? If it weren't for their son, he would have been miles away, is all he told himself these days. Of course, he omitted the part of his fiscal scarcity, which had forcefully kept his mouth shut and his eyes turned. He preferred not to go in that direction and instead chose to pat himself for being a good father and tolerating the cruelties for his son's sake.

He waited for a week, and then his patience started to wean off, and he headed to Urvi's house. Something would come out of the visit; he was confident after all the girls were synced to each other in every sphere. They were like two peas in a pod.

"Hey, where is Mols? I haven't seen her in over a week."

Was what he heard as soon as the door was opened to him. Seeing him a little bit taken aback and non-responsive, Urvi added, "Is she okay? Her phone comes switched off and messages go undelivered. It's just not like her." She paused and waited.

Sam waited, too. He was trying to figure out the authenticity of Urvi's concern and complaint. Was she playing or teasing him? Or was Urvi, in reality, unaware of what was going on? Had Molina carried on with her crusade all by herself? He had come here in the hope of getting the know-how of Molina and her disappearance. If she wasn't aware of Molina's current status quo, then he'd rather turn back and leave. He had faced too much humiliation all these months and didn't want to add more to it.

"I myself was not in town last few days. Just got back and since Mols was not home, I came here thinking she must be hanging out with you guys," he lied to save face. "She has too much on her hands these days. I am sure something must have kept her too busy to revert. Will pass on your concern to her as I see her." He didn't wait for any further dialogue and he left.

***

Molina spent her entire week in absolute panic and uncertainty. The magnitude of the step she took was finally descending on her now that she was all alone in an unacquainted city amongst unfamiliar people. She had packed off Veer to his grandparents and had slipped out one early morning as soon as she realized her day had arrived. She had felt a slight wave-like, mildly painful shiver, and she had started packing. It was around three in the morning, so she quietly managed to do it without alarming Sam. She had done the mental packing long back and just had to physically put it all together. She put some clothes in a separate bag for her son, put his school stuff and other essentials in it, and woke him up at around half past five. Half-asleep, he followed her out the door and into the cab. A short drive later, he was standing outside his grandparents' entrance, and in the silence of the early morning stillness, a loud-sounding doorbell announced his presence there. Molina waited across the road to see him being received by safe hands, and then she drove off. There was no note stuck to the child to explain this unexpected visit, nor was anyone left at home to explain his exit. Everything was open for interpretation and it was done to cause the kind of stir that Molina needed. Sam's parents were still in the dark about the upheaval in his marital life. So his confused father, who was subjected to this puzzling sight, made a concerned call to Sam.

Not having any knowledge of the incident, Sam was caught unawares. While he fumbled his excuses and took time to cook up a convincing response, he finally managed the last-minute emergency tour theory and put the phone down. To his relief, he knew the excitement of having the kid to stay over was enough to keep their other suspicions at bay.

This was the same excuse that Sam found handy when Urvi interrogated him about Molina's absence.

Urvi knew her delivery date had arrived and it was very likely that she had taken off. There was no way she could have the baby in this town. Not with what it was planned for and not with what would become of it.

Urvi knew now exactly where she could be, but she also knew that she was not going to be reachable. Her phone would be lying somewhere switched off and hidden. She needed to be untraceable and undisclosed. She needed anonymity and secrecy. It was decided that Molina had to eventually venture out on her own, as Urvi, with a newborn baby, was not a suitable accomplice. All the details of her whereabouts were given to Urvi just in case Molina took longer to reappear than planned, but the day and time were left upon nature.

With all the planning and preparations so well in advance and every detail well thought of, it didn't occur to her that being on her own for the culmination of her plot was going to be so daunting and unnerving. She spent the whole week in torture and turmoil. Her labour pain was not as bad, but it lasted long. The baby took too long to come out, as if refusing to be a part of this saga. And finally, she had to have a cesarean delivery. That meant more time recuperating. Her desire to get over and done with it hung in the air, and lying on the hospital bed, she had time to reminisce. She thought about the day it all began and about her constantly changing arguments about what she would do with the havoc she faced. Accepting it and living with it was not an option.

In her opinion, it wasn't supposed to be for any woman.

She felt extremely strongly about the unfairness of this widely accepted and oft repeated offence and was very clear that she would never ever support this arrangement for herself or otherwise.

She thought of many other ways to bring her husband to book and bring him to the same level of pain and suffering, but everything weighted in his favour. If she decided to leave him, she would give a broken home to her son, and Sam, being an absolutely involved and devoted father, she couldn't take that caring hand off her child. It also meant leaving the field clear for the gold digger to not only continue playing her game but actually hand her the victory trophy, too. She had worked hard to build a home for her family, and no flash in the pan was claiming it as her turf. No child was coming anywhere near what was her son's – emotional or financial. She would stay put for her kid and guard it with her life. And that ideally worked for Sam. Under the circumstances, his intact, uninterrupted family was all he could ask for. Anything under this roof, as long as it was the same roof and they were all under it together.

If Sam wanted to leave, he could gather the courage and leave. She knew he couldn't. With his misadventure in the picture, it was very unlikely that he would have had much of a future as a custodian and with Molina's fury at work, not much of a visitation possibility. Sam just had to eat what was served to him.

But that wasn't enough to keep her sane. She needed to drag him to where she was, bruised, broken and bleeding. Make a mockery of his guts and his greed. She wanted to strip him of his pride and leave him with a wound so deep that he would spend his lifetime nursing it.

And she found what she was looking for.

***

The length she had gone to seek her revenge was finally at its fag end, but the journey had extracted every ounce of strength out of her, and she was ready to fold.

One last stop.

She looked at those hazel-coloured eyes, and a victorious smile formed on her face. What are the odds, she thought? The hazel eyes were a cherry on the cake. Sam would spend his lifetime trying to figure out where these eyes came from. Who did they belong to? Molina could visualize Sam scrutinizing every man with eyes of the same colour, finding a possibility of their contribution. The eyes were going to hurt his eyes, and she dearly held the baby with the punishing eyes firmly in her arms and silently thanked her. What a beautiful girl. Just who she used to dream about. Her own baby girl and a sister of his own for her Veer.

When she was in turmoil over how she would buy back her happiness, peace and dignity after being stabbed in the back by Sam, the answer came in black and white on the fifth page of the daily national newspaper. An NGO was sheltering the young pregnancies of teenage, unwed mothers and rape victims by giving them a safe place and required medical assistance and later setting up those unwanted babies for adoption. The initiative was not only praiseworthy but could be supported, too. It fulfilled many of her desires. She had been keen to have a sibling for her son, but with her marriage on the rocks, she knew she wouldn't be able to have her own. She also had always wanted to adopt, and if she chose to go for it, she could get to have both.

She had contacted an NGO and did the necessary inquiries about the procedure. After raising and satisfying her concerns about the secrecy of the identity of both biological and adoptive mothers, she was assured that it was legit and trustworthy. All she had to do was to send in her requirements, if she had any, regarding religious and race preference. They didn't want any baby rejected or neglected on any account. She just had one preference. She wanted a girl child.

With that deal done, Molina carried on with her original plan to appear pregnant. She searched for couples looking for surrogacy. It would help someone's dream to have a child come true, and it would help give the desired pain and anguish to her husband. It was a nightmarish sight for any man to see his wife walk around carrying someone else's child in his own house. She would flaunt her baby bump as a sign of disloyalty to Sam, just as that woman of his was flaunting his disloyalty to her. She would do that to him and much more. It would be a very noble act on her part, and it would make the journey so much more enriching and satisfying.

She had spent the last nine months tending to her pregnancy as one would to a lifesaving device. This baby was going to do for her what nothing else could. Then, after giving birth, she would hand over the baby to its biological parents, and she would go and adopt. She would deliver one baby and bring home another.

A perfect plan for a perfect revenge, in which it was just win-win for her.

***

She signed the adoption papers, made the authorities sign the non-discloser agreement, said thank you, and with her daughter in her arms, she left.

All she needed was to return home holding a baby and a baby it was. A beautiful, sweet little hazel-eyed doll of a girl.

She looked at those eyes and then looked up at the sky. A wide smile spread across her face, and her eyes lit up.

Even she couldn't have planned it better.

God was in sync with her, she knew.

And with her dignity and integrity intact, for her, this was the only way it could have been undone.

ACKNOWLEDGEMENTS

TO MY HUSBAND

Thank you for constantly encouraging and never doubting, and thank you for your unconditional support. This book would not have been possible without you.

TO MS SHOBHA DE

Thank you for taking the time out of your busy schedule to read the entire work of a novice like me and giving your encouraging nod. Eternally obliged.

TO ARUP BOSE AND SRISHTI PUBLISHERS

Thank you for giving me the opportunity to present my work to the world. For being the most easy going and appreciative team ever. It was a pleasure to work with you.